Death at
Island Life

Death at
Island Life

§

DONOLD KING LOURIE

Library of Congress Number:		2001119536
ISBN #:	Hardcover	1-4010-3804-2
	Softcover	1-4010-3803-4

To order additional copies of this book, contact:
Xlibris Corporation
1-888-7-XLIBRIS
www.Xlibris.com
Orders@Xlibris.com

Samantha

CHAPTER ONE

T homas Granville Farrington went into cardiac arrest on the lat-pull. I didn't need 911 to tell me what the problem was. Or whether he'd live, for that matter.

He'd been hyperactive that morning, yanking the T-row like a twenty year old. He demanded fifteen extra pounds on his bench press. His bicep curls were fast and abrupt. His eyes bulged, his head snapped like a drummer gone wild.

I put a hand on his thin shoulder. "Maybe you'd better take a breather, Tommy." Then I whispered in his ear, "Or a nitro!"

I don't know why I whispered. No one else was in the weight room and no one upstairs could have heard me, the hard rock being what it is at Island Life. Besides, I knew he wouldn't take any advice from a woman. He was that sort of man.

He gasped, said he wanted 30 additional pounds on the lat-pull. He was groaning out his second set and I was counting, "eleven, good; twelve, wonderful; thirteen . . ."

He suddenly looked up at me in amazement, the bar trembled in his hands. "What the . . . errr," he gargled. Then he vomited forward, over the frame of the machine.

His liver-spotted hands were still gripping the bar. It lifted him to his feet and, for a moment, he stared at me as though I'd stuck a knife in his back.

"You berritch!" he gasped, his gray beard dripping.

There was hatred and terror in those dying blue eyes of his. He knew how and why he was dying.

And I'll admit something to you right now. I'd dreamed about this moment. I'd seen it happen over and over again. I'd even planned how to make it happen.

But now it was the real thing and it wasn't satisfying, not one damn bit. I'd never seen anyone die. I guess it was the terror in his eyes that got to me. I could take the hatred.

I was dizzy, clammy with sweat. I thought I'd be sick. I reached out to him. "Oh Tommy, let me help you!"

He pushed me aside. Clawing at his chest, he staggered out the door and down the hall. I was right behind him. His thin white hair waved in the air as he lurched along.

At the foot of the stairs, he clutched for the rails on both sides, hauled himself up, one trembling step after the other. Thank heaven I didn't follow him. When he got to the top, his back to me, he straightened, raised his arms high in the air. Then, like a stunt double in a grade B movie, he toppled backward, his rigid body bumping almost all the way down the stairs.

At the top, I could hear Jo Ellen screaming. A tom-tom beat in my head, my eyes blurred. His head, I noticed, had taken its last bounce on the fifth step from the bottom. And yes, later rumors were true. He had one whopper of a hard-on.

I'll tell you about the fifth step in a minute. But I'm admitting right now that I knew something about that hard-on. After all, I knew the old man pretty well. I'd been his trainer—and more—for over twenty years. In my business you get to know a hell of a lot about your clients, like them or not.

I'm not trying to be funny when I say his boner was a big island item for a while. No, the *Mirror*, our weekly newspaper, didn't mention it. Didn't have to, really. By evening most of the island had heard about

Tommy Farrington's last erection. Ours is a small island. News travels fast.

So there he was, head down, pecker up on my newly carpeted stairs. And there I was, stunned with fear. I knew damn well there wasn't a chance in hell of bringing him around. So while my staff—Jo Ellen and Donnie Kay—began yanking Tommy back up the stairs, I called the cops, then Barbara Farrington, Tommy's wife.

She got to Island Life before the cops did. I'd talked to her maid who must have called Barbara's car phone. Anyway, when Barbara came through my door and saw her husband's body, her beautiful face went pale. It went crimson when she noticed that erection of his. It had lifted his red sweats like the center pole of an Indian teepee.

I wondered if she knew Tommy never wore a jock strap under his sweats. I also wondered whether she could guess how much he'd told me about his sex life and how much he liked being naked in my sunroom.

According to Tommy, he'd been telling her for years his arteries and heart were too weak for sex. But maybe he hadn't told me the truth. Maybe he'd found out about Barbara and Father Berry even before the rumor got started. I'd heard the rumor from one of my more reliable clients. But then, there have always been rumors about Ralph Berry.

I'll say right up front that I've never liked him. He's too nice, too clean and good. Swiss cheese holy, if you know what I mean. The times I've talked to him—usually when my husband has been in trouble—I've found him sort of unreal. Along with that handsome face and soothing voice, there's a creepy, like-to-convert-you look in his eyes.

Maybe I just imagined that look. You see there's talk that when he prays at the bedside of certain parishioners, his hands get pretty fidgety in the Lord's work. Especially when the sick woman is under sixty and religious as all hell.

Marsha Elder, one of my best clients, says the rumors are untrue. She works at the police station. She's married to Sam Elder who goes off his rocker now and then and has to be put away. She's very devout and forty-five and of course she gets pretty sad when Sam's locked up.

She tells me Ralph Berry is right there when she needs him, no fidgety hands, just good Christian love and understanding.

But on that subject, there's another interesting fact. After Father Berry's wife died, he gave that very controversial sermon on the role of the Holy Ghost in true love. Apparently he went so far as to say that you could get a real good feel of the Holy Ghost in sexual climax. You could get an even better feel if you were Episcopalian. Of course he was talking about married love. But it made a lot of people wonder.

When it comes to sex, you never know. Fact can be what you want to hear or won't hear. For a for-instance, take my own husband. I have an idea what Budgy Hill does when he's on tour. But I don't want to know for sure. Of course nobody's going to talk to me about it. If they did, I'd just say I didn't believe them, that's all.

But I know that after the grunting and groaning is over, after the spinning heel kicks, headlocks, and pile drivers, Budgy no doubt could do it with as many of those little starry-eyed fans as he's still got strength for. Which isn't a whole lot, I'm sure. But little girl fans love professional wrestlers' big bodies. And Budgy loves little girls.

Well that's not quite right. Budgy likes to fuck little girls. But he truly loves only me, always has, always will. I can't tell you how much he depends on me and how many times he's kicked the living shit out of guys who come on to me in bars.

But back to Tommy. My call to the police had gotten me Chick Vado and another cop I didn't know. Signed on for the summer, I supposed. I did know Chick all right. Everyone, including me, thinks he is probably the dumbest cop on our force. He'd screwed up the Mary Jane Houston case some three years before and got our island a lot of national attention. Laughing attention. Why he didn't get fired, I'll never know. But that's another story altogether.

Anyhow, when Chick Vado strutted into my place, he looked around at everyone like they were under suspicion. "No one," he said importantly, "leaves here until I say so." He looked darkly at me. "You're the director of this establishment, are you not?"

"Jesus, Chick! No. I was just passing through town. I mean, who you trying to impress?"

For the first time, he looked down at Tommy. Casually, as though he'd seen a million corpses. "That's the body, I presume. Just answer the . . . What's that," his voice trailed off, "sticking up?" He looked at me, his face red as a beet. He looked quickly back at the body. "Maybe he's . . . not dead."

And just that moment–I swear to God–Tommy's teepee trembled. Maybe there was a draft, someone coming through the door. But I don't think so. Very few were looking down at the body, but I heard a gasp or two and a shriek. When I turned around I saw that Barbara Farrington had fainted.

So five minutes later there was more than just a stiff for Dr. Sponge Langor to look at. We have three physicians on the island and Sponge is my favorite. There are stories about all three of them, but Sponge is supposed to have gotten his name from leaving a sponge in one of his patients.

"Interesting," he said after a quick examination of Tommy. "Dead, all right." He stood up. "Happens when people are hanged," he said, looking at the teepee.

We had gotten Barbara onto the sofa. She had come to, but covered her face while Sponge was examining her husband. When he examined her she started to cry, said she was fine. Was there anything that could be done for Tommy?

Sponge shook his head, felt her pulse, and told her she'd be all right but to stay on the sofa awhile. In the meantime, Chick and the other cop were getting Tommy into a body bag–with some difficulty, I might add.

When that was over, Chick took the names, addresses, and telephone numbers of everyone present. Even mine! "Chick," I whispered, "what the hell? Tommy died of a heart attack. What's all this detective crap?"

"No comment," he whispered mysteriously and went on collecting information. After that he told everyone except Sponge to be back in my place at three that same afternoon.

I stayed around until they got Tommy out my door and into the ambulance Chick had called for. Then I closed the club and went home for a belt of Jack Daniel's and a ham sandwich. Budge was away, which was good. I could do a little heavy thinking, undisturbed.

While I was home, Chick phoned to tell me the Chief had put him on the Farrington case, and he wanted the club closed while he questioned my clients that afternoon.

"What *case*?" I hollered at him. "Farrington died of a heart attack. What's all the fuss about?"

Chick lowered his voice. "Our business," he said.

All right, so it was going to be a case. But why Chick Vado? A bad sign. I thought I could weather it, probably. But it made me even more upset. Why hadn't Chief Joey Horne put himself on the case? Joey and I were friends, sort of. We'd fooled around years ago. That was before my Budgy, of course, and before Joey decided teenage boys were his preference and got his divorce from May.

I and the Chief—he was just a Corporal then—had our laughs. Mostly about the way he liked to come off, all dressed up like he did. Naturally I told him he was lovely. And he truly got to believe whatever he did with me or anyone else was okay.

He was grateful, thought I'd straightened him out, sexwise. He owed me, you see, and if there was going to be a case on Tommy's death, I wanted Joey, not Chick, on it.

It wasn't only that Chick Vado was stupid. His real name isn't Chick. It's Chinkway, not Chick. Chinkway means five in Italian. He was the fifth son of one of the Boston Vados. But the point of this is that I'm superstitious about fives.

As a for-instance, I don't ever think of myself having five fingers on my hand or five toes on a foot. I have ten fingers and I have ten toes. That'll tell you how bad it is. And when Tommy's head landed on that fifth step of mine I was scared shitless. Almost anything terrible can happen when fives are involved.

I suppose you want to know how I got that way. Briefly, I mean. No Freudian crapola.

It was like this. My father used to beat on my mother. Regularly, to celebrate Friday night when his work week was over. Friday's the fifth day of the week, right? But it's much worse than that. Once, when I tried to stop him, he took the buckle end of a belt to me. It crushed my fifth vertebra.

Later, on May 5, 1975, I was sentenced to the Worcester prison for not three, not four, but five years. Five fucking years for selling one gram of coke. Which wasn't true! So help me God, I was using it with a friend. At least I thought he was a friend until he lied and said I sold it to him.

Well, there's more about fives. But you get the idea. So when Chick, real name Chinkway, got put on the Farrington case, I freaked out. Maybe Joey put him on it because he'd answered the 911. I don't know. But that afternoon he came swaggering into Island Life like he was ten feet tall. I can tell you that he's a skinny little guy who still wears his hair long like in the sixties. The way he gets big is by giving orders and making everyone uncomfortable.

The first thing he did was to make us, one by one, sit in the sunroom and answer his stupid questions. The sunroom's the ultraviolet room for tanning. No windows, a small cot, a chair, walls painted all around like the beach at Waikiki.

The reason we each had to sit down was because he's so fucking short he can't get his head higher than yours unless you're sitting and he's standing. Everyone had to tell Chick exactly what they were doing just before they heard Jo Ellen scream.

I asked Chick to go easy on Jo Ellen. She was crying most of the morning. She's just a high school kid, pimples and all. When she saw old Tommy with his hands up and his dick pointing her way, then saw him fall backward down the stairs, she got the fright of her life. We could hear her sobbing through the sunroom door. From now on she's going to have a hard time—if you'll excuse the expression—with most sexual activities.

After Chick got finished with the questioning, he ordered us to take the same places we were in and to be doing just what we were doing when Jo Ellen screamed. Florence Eddy had been in the bathroom. By Jesus if I didn't think Chick was going to make her take her pants down!

So for Chick I had to do the lat-pull myself, counting all over again.

"Eleven, twelve . . . thirteen," I said, trying not to hear Tommy groaning or see the bald spot in the center of his ratty white hair.

"Yeah. And then?" Chick asked me when I stopped counting.

"Barf, splash!" I said, waving my hand from my mouth toward the spine of the machine so, possibly, Vado'd get the full picture.

But he just stood there, mouth open, eyes narrowing, nodding wisely like he was Sherlock Holmes. "Adds up, don't it?" He stuck a big wad of Doublemint in his mouth and asked me to go down the hall and up the stairs like Tommy did.

"Yeah," Chick said, chewing that gum louder and faster as I pulled my way up the stairs. He'd stayed at the bottom, like I had. "You could be in the movies!" he said.

When I reached the top, I raised my arms in the air. "Yeah, yeah! Adds up, don't it? Go on, go on!"

Everyone was watching me. I was sweating bullets, getting dizzy as hell from seeing it all over again. I couldn't help it. I lifted my face to the ceiling and yelled, "Wait a god damn minute, Chick, you dumb dago! What the fuck's this all about?" I whirled around—I can get pretty explosive—and hollered down the stairs. "You think I'm gonna do Farrington's fall? Fuck you! I'll tell you what happened for the twentieth time and you do the fall! And I'll also tell you this. If you crack that lead head of yours going down, you'll pay me for what it does to my stairs!"

I suppose he didn't like my ethnic reference much. I was sorry about that. But I'd had enough. And I wasn't so confused I didn't see the afternoon crowd coming from the beaches and gathering outside my door. College kids mostly. Summer people. Summer Tanners we call them. Late summer afternoons are the only time Island Life makes real money.

I walked down the stairs and told Chick to get the hell out of my club and not come back unless he had a warrant to close me down. What the hell was he doing, I said again, this time maybe a little louder than before. Was there some sort of crime when a man dies from a good old-fashioned heart attack?

Chick sputtered around. But he left the club and didn't come back with a warrant to close me down. What he did come back with was much, much worse.

CHAPTER TWO

I had my usual breakfast at the Flake. Orange juice, coffee with three spoonfuls of sugar, two eggs sunny side up, two glazed doughnuts. Too much, I suppose. But in police work you've got to be ready for anything. Including not getting any lunch or supper when there's a big case going. And maybe the Farrington case would be a big one.

I hoped so. It might be, just might be, my chance for a comeback. I hadn't been able to sleep last night and, thinking about it now, I got so nervous I had a second cigarette. I'd screwed up the Houston case, digging up that old Indian grave and telling everyone we'd found Jane Houston, the woman who'd disappeared here on the island. I'd been pretty embarrassed.

I crossed the cobblestone street to the station. Thinking so hard, I darn near fell. What a nuisance, those cobblestones. They're supposed to make our town look like it did in the whaling days, the stones being ballast on ships returning from voyages around the world.

Bunk! My mind goes on it this way. If the returning ships had whale oil in their big casks, why did they need ballast? It's the story for the tourists and I don't bring up the obvious objection. Don't want to embarrass anyone. After all that's happened. And in my line of work, I've always tried to keep a low profile.

I love this island. Along the street the clapboard and shingle storefronts have window boxes of petunias and daisies. Very pretty. But the street turns even better and more serious when you get to my part of it. The firehouse, the courthouse and the municipal building are red brick. Solid, orderly, signs of strength.

The police department takes up most of the first floor of the municipal building. Joey wanted window boxes but we kidded him out of them. For a tough cop—and he's really tough—he has some crazy ideas. Like those silk handkerchiefs he wears in his uniform pocket. Like that greenhouse he spends his free time in, taking care of his flowers and other things.

I knocked on his door and went in. His feet were on his desk. He was smoking a cigarette through that long ivory holder of his. The one with the scrimshaw of the naked lady on it.

"Well now, Vado. Good to see you. Thought you might be taking the day off."

Joey likes to kid around. Knows darn well my day off is Tuesday. "Just having my usual breakfast, Chief."

"Not exactly a usual day though, is it? Possible murder on our hands. But what the hell, breakfasts are important, right?"

"You got it, Chief."

He studied me for a moment, grabbed for that handkerchief. "Well I'm glad that's cleared up." He sneezed into it and put it back in his breast pocket. I don't like to think of the germs in that pocket!

"Maybe," Joey said, "you'd better tell me what exactly you found out yesterday afternoon."

"Questioned everyone in the club. Except Farrington of course." I like to kid around myself. But Joey didn't laugh. Strange sense of humor, Joey. "I talked to his doc, though. And here's the way my mind has been going on it. You could say everything I heard adds up. History of heart problems, taking medications, vigorous workout, increased weights on the lat-pull, age eighty-two. Except for Hettie Hill, no one near the old man when he had the attack. Bingo. Heart attack for sure!"

I put my hand out to stop Joey's question. "On the other hand, we've got the telegram. And we've got a lot of people in this town who hated the victim. You can't ignore that kind of hatred, can you?"

"Anything else?" Horne asked. "This file maybe?" He shoved the file toward me.

I'd looked at the file last night. On the top, of course, was the telegram. It had been sent the night before, but we'd received it at the station an hour before I answered the 911 from Island Life. FARRINGTON WILL DIE HARD was what it said. It was the reason why I'd had to question all those folks at Island Life and take those insults from Hettie.

We'd traced it to a phone in a vacant house in Burlington, Vermont. The house had been broken into and the sender had charged the overnight telegram to the credit card of the absent owner of the house.

While I studied the telegram, Horne sneezed again. I closed my eyes while he put the handkerchief back. Disgusting. "This word 'hard,'" I said, "seems darn important to me."

Discerning a smile of approval on Joey's face, I said, "Glad you agree. We've got to deal with that . . . ah . . . condition of the victim, don't we? I mean, considering the way this telegram is worded?" I was a little embarrassed so I added, "Sponge says people have them when they get hanged. We could look into that, I suppose."

Joey asked me through his teeth if by any chance I thought Farrington had been hanged. And when, naturally, I shook my head, he asked if I'd read the rest of the file. Actually, he said the *fucking* rest of the file. He can get pissed off and vulgar for very little reason. I leafed through it quickly. Mostly reports from the 911s we had from the Farrington place over the years. I'd answered a couple of them myself. One time the Farrington dogs damn near ate me alive. Mrs. Farrington had seen an intruder or a peeping Tom. Why are women always seeing peeping Toms? But—as I said in my report on it—who would want to peep at Mrs. Farrington, as pretty as she is, with those vicious wiremongers on guard duty?

There was a rumor her husband starved those seven or eight dogs, put raw meat on the top of a big pole he tied them to. When he went to bed or made a trip somewhere, he took the meat away and turned the dogs loose on his fifty-five acres.

It was all fenced in—electrically, of course—right down to the beach. Last summer a college long-distance swimmer came in there for a rest and one of the dogs took his foot off at the ankle. Tells you about the dangers of swimming, doesn't it? I personally don't swim much. A lot of us native islanders don't see the value in it.

The Chief was getting restless. He took his feet off the desk and stamped them down hard on the floor. "Any chance you've found Rodney's last report?"

I didn't say anything.

"Christ!" he said. "Let me help you then. Rodney's report says Farrington's missus told Rodney, as late as last Tuesday night, that someone was trying to kill her husband."

I remembered that report but my mental processes had gone this way on it. Like I said, we had plenty of false alarms from the Farrington place. Every time I answered the 911, Mrs. Farrington would get off the peeping Tom excuse and tell me how so many people hated her husband and were trying to get back at him by hurting her. Even with the dogs, she was afraid for her life.

So this recent report of Rodney's was just one of many and I figured he'd probably got it wrong. I like Rodney Jar—funny name, eh?—but he's probably the dumbest cop I ever worked with. He'd most likely gotten it wrong. She was afraid for *her* life, not her husband's. That's the way my mind went on it.

Furthermore, I myself didn't share the hate everyone had for Thomas G. Farrington. I admit, it was easy, maybe natural, not to like him. Very few people did. Most of the town called him a prick, which is interesting, isn't it? I mean considering his condition at death. I made a quick mental note to talk to Joey about that at the right moment in the future of the case.

Even almost everyone on the force hated Tommy. There was talk that maybe the Chief got darn nice Christmas presents—green ones— from Farrington. But I knew that didn't stop Joey from hating the man.

Some said you had to be deaf, dumb, and blind to like the old man.

About five years ago he'd built the biggest house on the island: gardens, swimming pool, tennis court, caretaker's house, greenhouse, stable, five-car garage. All that work, plus a gardener, a cook, and a maid provided good money for the island. But he treated most islanders like—excuse the expression—horse manure. Nothing ever got done to his satisfaction. His usual reaction to what anyone did for him was, "Another island fuck up! What am I doing with a tribe of Neanderthals on a fifth-rate God-forsaken sandbar?" Something like that. And he'd say it right in the faces of the people working for him.

But I have to tell you something. I felt sorry for Mr. Farrington. I know what it is to be disliked. Sometimes it's worse than being laughed at. And I've had both. I mean you never know if you've got the right facts. Nobody did when I arrested that FBI man during the Houston case. But most everyone here hated me. We were a laughing stock in the national newspapers. Then it was all brought up at a town meeting, and when I stood up to defend myself, I was booed and laughed at so much I didn't get to say a thing.

People didn't have the full story on that business and maybe we didn't have the full story on Mr. Farrington. Like maybe he had a disease he knew would kill him one day. Maybe he was always in a lot of pain. Or maybe he knew people didn't like him and that made him angry. With everyone against him, he was someone you could feel sorry for.

But what was he doing on our island? That was what most people wondered, too. He'd been a Summer Tanner here for years and years while he was making a fortune in business. Doing what? No one knew for sure. Something about clothespins. A wheeler dealer, I guess. Buying everyone out, cornering the market.

Joey was running his slender hand over his bald head. "Autopsy?" he asked.

"Coffin does them," I said.

"I know who does them, for God's sake. The question is whether to ask for one."

"You're the Chief," I said. When he runs his hand like that over his bald head, I know he's thinking out loud and it's better not to interrupt him.

He closed his eyes. "Think of the work we'll have, all the attention—maybe even the Bureau again—if, say, there's poison in his gut, or some god damn thing like that."

He didn't say anything for a while. Finally he told me to get out to the Farrington place and see if I could get Mrs. Farrington's okay for an autopsy. It was the decision I would have made from the beginning.

Driving out to North Point was a pleasure that almost made me forget the dogs I'd have to deal with. From the road I could spot the green sea through the dunes and scrub oak. In the wind the breakers glistened like mounds of white cotton candy. I could hear their boom over the sound of my engine. Rosa rugosa and beach plum lined parts of the road. I wondered whether God or the selectmen had planted all that color there for the tourists to see. It didn't matter. What a beautiful island I live on.

But in police work you have to keep your mind on your job. I recalled several important details of the last forty-eight hours. In my line you got to have good recall. First I remembered Mrs. Farrington on the sofa watching me and Rodney getting Farrington into that body bag. We were having one heck of a time with his condition, I mean getting it flat so we could zip up the bag. First time I ever had a problem like that, I'll tell you!

But I didn't let the problem stop me from keeping an eye on the reactions of all the witnesses. I noticed how Mrs. Farrington kept putting her hand over her face and crying when she thought I was looking at her. Sometimes that kind of behavior can tell you a lot.

Then there were Hettie's reactions. She's not my type, physically or mentally, I mean. Physically, she's wiry, even scrawny from the knees up. But she has these muscles on her calves like summer squashes. Her face is all angles, with a high forehead she covers with her bangs. I've seen those dark bangs flipping up and down when she's out jogging on our bicycle paths. She's a beautiful runner.

Her tongue is too sharp for me, too. She has a take on everyone and it's usually bitter, vinegary even. She was always clever and a little mean like that, even as a kid. Full of energy, take the head off of anyone who contradicted her. For example, she loves cats. When I said I hated them, she said I didn't know my something from first base. I can't really repeat the something.

She's one of those revved-up health nuts, too. Runs x number of miles per week, vegetarian, gallons of water every day. So I wasn't surprised when she opened a health club for other health nuts.

Cost money, that club. Nautilus equipment, weights, aerobics classes. Makes a pile of money off the Summer Tanners. She makes even more as a private trainer. Fifty or sixty bucks an hour. She doesn't do very much, either. Just stands beside them and counts and tells them "good job!" or "strong today!" Things like that.

But I like her, I confess it. She's pretty, in her own way. And she's brave, too. After all, it takes nerve to start a new business like that when everyone is healthy to start with. A health club on a healthy island? Who needs it?

But most of all I like her because she's up front, so to speak. I'm like that myself, except when I'm on duty. The way I see it is, if a cop is up front on a case, it's not a case.

Of course she was nasty to me yesterday and I was pretty sore about that. She likes me, always has, I think. But I suppose she thought I was asking her to fall down the stairs like poor old Farrington. The "fucking" stairs, she called them. I'm not into that kind of talk. And she called me a dago. Which was intended to hurt me, I suppose. But it really didn't. What the heck, I'm of Italian descent. So what's to hurt? But she intended to hurt me and that hurt.

Being an officer of the law and thinking about her reaction, my thought processes went like this on it: Hettie Hill is tough and cool. So why'd she blow up like that? She'd overreacted during my routine investigation. If there was more to Farrington's death than meets the eye, she might herself be seriously involved. Which would be bad, real bad. As maybe you can tell, I think I may have loved her, secretly I mean, for a long time.

And there's something else I should say. Don't like to, but it's true. When I said she was a health nut, I didn't mean she was pure. I knew she played around. Always did in high school. And marrying Budge Hill maybe hadn't stopped her. What she saw in Budge I sure didn't know and still don't. He's a tub of muscle, particularly in his brain. Always jealous of anyone she spends any time with, men or women. And he gets into terrible brawls. Takes four of us–half the summer force–to control him.

But like I say, she did play around a lot. To tell the truth, I always thought it possible she had done it once or twice with Joey Horne when he had my job years ago. And now it came to me that maybe she'd been doing something with Farrington when he was on that lat-pull. I doubt it, but how else do you explain that condition of his?

I hated myself for thinking about Hettie that way. But Mr. Farrington was rich as creases and girls go for that kind of money and power. As I said, Farrington was big in clothespins. Not just the ordinary kind, either. The story was that he'd made millions, lost everything, gone bankrupt, recovered, made millions again. Never seemed to give up or run completely out of money. He was one of the first Summer Tanners to have a private jet. And with this new house of his he had a helicopter pad and a speedboat he could lower into the ocean from a crane that rolled down the beach.

When he built here, we expected he'd continue to be a Summer Tanner only, spend the rest of the year in Florida or the Caribbean. But he didn't do that. He married the fourth Mrs. Farrington and stuck it out here through our dark winters. Just what he did all day was a mystery. And now I suppose we'll never know.

The big gate was open and I drove right in. My windows were rolled up tight and the doors locked. I wasn't taking any chances on the dogs. I could have telephoned that I was coming out. But surprise is a good thing in my line of work.

When I got to the white clamshell circle in front of the house, I parked by the front door and leaned on the horn. I realized I was losing some of the surprise, but I have my priorities when it comes to being torn apart by hungry dogs.

After awhile Mrs. Farrington came out with Father Berry. "What are you doing?" she shouted through the rolled up window. I could see she'd been grieving. In this business you notice everything. Her face was pale. Her blond hair hung loose behind her back, out of its usual bun. Father, too, looked pale and somber. He's mostly a happy, pink-faced man. I could see right then that comforting the bereaved can take its toll. Father Berry is a good priest, been doing wonders here for years.

I got out of the car slowly, keeping my eyes and ears open for the dogs. "Sorry about the horn," I said, shaking hands with them both. I tried to make it a joke, "The wiremongers don't always know the police are friendly."

"The what?" Mrs. Farrington asked. I'd forgotten how pretty she was. Dimpled cheeks and breasts like grapefruits. Her blouse was unbuttoned a little which took my mind off the dogs for a minute.

"What's that?" I asked.

"Who doesn't know the police are friendly?" she asked.

I looked around the yard again. "Your dogs," I said, "the wiremongers."

She smiled at Father. "I see. Well, I've penned them up. Nothing to be afraid of. Fair, my husband, never penned them. He liked them to run at night. He was so . . ." She couldn't finish the sentence and I could see from her trembling lips she was going to cry.

Father gave her arm a squeeze and she said, "I remember you now. You're Officer Vado. How is your hand?" She reached for it and the three of us stared at the four little yellow marks where the teeth had gone through the skin and into the bones.

"Beastly dogs!" Father said.

"Put their teeth into my arm and leg. If you'd like to see it." I started to unbutton my jacket to get at my belt.

"Not necessary, at all," Mrs. Farrington said. She was too nice for ugly sights, I figured. Just then she caught me looking at her cleavage. Some color came back to her face. Buttoning up her blouse, she asked me why I'd come all this way without calling.

I told her that for reasons of our own, we thought an autopsy of her husband might be advisable, that we wanted her approval.

"An autopsy?" she looked astonished. "Whatever for? You can ask Dr. Field about my husband's heart condition. He was eighty-two, after all."

I told her I'd already spoken to Dr. Field–he's another of our doctors on the island–and we still thought an autopsy was advisable.

"You suspect foul play?" Father asked.

I kept my mouth shut, of course, studied them both for a half minute. Silence in a police officer can get results. And even if it doesn't, it's intimating. You can go on with a certain advantage.

"Well, I won't have it!" Mrs. Farrington said. "Cutting his body all up like that." She began to cry.

Father Berry put an arm around her shoulders and said to me, "Now look here, Chuck." He always gets my name wrong. "You know what happened at Island Life. Is there any reason to believe it was more than a simple heart attack?"

I couldn't tell him about the telegram without Horne's okay. So I had to think pretty fast. "You're right, Father. Heart attack's been my hypotheosis all along."

Father didn't seem to know the word. "My original premise," I said. I would have thought a man like Father Berry would have heard, at least on television, how the police talk about a case. He seemed embarrassed so I decided to let him in a little. "I'll be frank with you, Father. There have been threats, enemies perhaps."

"What threats?" Mrs. Farrington asked. "What enemies?" She looked pretty angry.

What the heck, I thought. She herself had complained to Rodney that someone was trying to kill her husband. When I want to keep silent but let people know I have answers, I simply raise my hand and then wave it vaguely in the air. The gesture can be pretty impressive.

"I think I'd better call my lawyer," Mrs. Farrington said, looking at Father. "Come with me, dear."

Father put a strong grip on my arm. "I hope you won't have to do it, Chuck. Some of us consider autopsy a desecration unless there's good cause. I shouldn't think you or your boss would want to get involved in something like that."

Before I could get a handle on the threatening tone in his voice, he had turned and followed Mrs. Farrington through the big front door. I did have time to holler as nicely as I could, "It's not Chuck, it's Chick!"

CHAPTER THREE

After Barbara wrangled with her lawyer, she broke down again. I managed to get her back on the sofa, tuck the afghan around her while she wept. "Oh God! What have I done, what have I done?"

She was on the same sofa, stretched out in the same way she had been before the arrival of the policeman. I had at that time been well on my way to easing her anguish. Her trust in me as faithful friend and confessor had even caused her to clutch my hand and lift her face to kiss me. It was a tribute she seemed instantly embarrassed about.

Let me set the scene for you. Barbara Farrington, one of the finest and dearest of my parishioners, learned by telephone yesterday that her husband had suddenly died. She had, as a matter of fact, seen his body wrapped and carried from the health club he often visited. She'd telephoned me this morning in utter despair and I'd found her in her bedroom on this very sofa.

I did what I could to comfort her. We prayed together while her maid brought us tea. Other than our communion wine, there is nothing like tea—with lemon and a bit of Sweet 'n Low —to open one's senses to the Lord. I told her as much and, of course, she smiled at the bit of humor in the comparison.

Although it caused her silently to weep, I reminded her of her past courage in facing and overcoming the many indignities she had suffered at the hands of her husband. She had more than once, tearfully and with the utmost reluctance, confessed to me how he had abused her.

"Oh, I know, I know!" she sobbed. "But I loved him so. I truly loved him. He couldn't help himself, you know. He could really never help himself!"

To soothe and appease her, I nodded and said, "I understand, of course. But you must put him, and all those memories, away from you." In all honesty I had never believed her husband was incapable of controlling his aggressive behavior toward her. From everything I knew about her—and it was quite a lot—I was certain she had always been, however tortured, a caring and obedient wife.

Just before the policeman arrived, she had put her anguished face again on the pillow. She was at that moment as lovely as I had ever seen her. I felt, of course, an overwhelming need to transmit to her the sweet peace of the Holy Ghost. "Dear Barbara," I said softly, "would you let me soothe your brow in this hour of your deep sorrow? You know from our work together how the spirit of the Lord has passed before from my soul to yours."

"Oh do, please," she whispered.

At that, I touched her forehead with the tips of my fingers, ran them slowly over her pale cheek and down her neck to her clavicle. Slowly and gently repeating this movement, I whispered the while, "May the love of God be with you, dearest Barbara."

By her closed eyes and the peaceful smile on her pretty lips, I knew she was content. With my thumb and fingers ever so lightly around her throat I said, "Now let the power of the Holy Spirit enter and possess you in this, your hour of need."

It was then that she had taken my hand from her neck, lifted her face to kiss my lips. In the quick movement of her shoulders, the two top buttons of her blouse came unfastened. But the sudden sound of the policeman's horn, as though it were God's warning, restrained my trembling hand.

So, as I've said, after we had dealt with the policeman—a truly unremarkable man named Chuck something or other—Barbara called her lawyer. She argued with him about the right of the police to perform an autopsy, then, overcome with grief, went back to her sofa.

"What have I done?" she sobbed. "What have I done?"

I remonstrated with her. She had done nothing wrong, been an exceptionally forgiving wife. She shook her head, cried out that she could have been so much more the woman he needed, given in to him more than she had. I made it clear to her that she had done all she could for her husband. Anything more would have been suicidal, knowing his aggressive personality. She then permitted me to stroke her head. Within minutes she was fast asleep.

God's ministry in a small parish has its hard work and its rewards. In general it is fascinating work. It can equal the challenge of the largest of our cities, filled as they are with so many sinners.

"Christians abound but sinners surround," to quote the wise and pithy words of Aloysius Blackbourne, one of our greatest eighteenth-century bishops. I have found it applicable everywhere.

And of course, there is always that even larger group of "inbetweeners," as I rather laughingly call them. I particularly like that term for use on an island such as this where humor and simple language are important. As I tell my parish, partly for their amusement, inbetweeners can be found—though they may not themselves know it—on that often pleasureful path between right and wrong, between good and evil, gratified one moment, guilty the next.

My goal, of course, is to spread the word of God and the teachings of Jesus. If the goal seems simple, the work is not. It involves every technique I've learned in my ministries—Chicago, Fort Wayne, Dubuque, and, finally, here on this most gorgeous of New England islands.

I should tell you, of course, that without the loving support of my adorable Nora, I would never have achieved my many successes. Especially here. She directed our little church school, edited and published *Jesus Speaks*, our church bulletin, found time to administer to most of my needs as priest and man. In addition to all this, she had an endearing way of becoming friend and companion to many of my flock.

Perhaps she was too close to some of them. Perhaps she over-worked for the Lord. I don't know. She certainly over-worried. A conscientious and anxious woman, she knew often—too often, I fear—of my exhausting efforts to comfort those in trouble. She fretted particularly over my untiring work in assuaging the cares of certain of the depressed women of my parish whose lives on this small island had become incredibly drear.

It all became, finally, too much for her and she took her life under very peculiar circumstances. God rest her soul. How dreadfully I missed her.

My loneliness after Nora's death was intense. I needn't remind you of those needs that cannot be met by work alone. You may, therefore, understand why in my ministry after Nora I was drawn to Barbara Farrington.

We have many beautiful women on this little island. She was, however, in some way different. She was soft-spoken with just a touch of southern accent. Sweet, rather delicate of body and temperament, she had—how could one fail to notice it—the figure of Aphrodite. I particularly liked the shape of her neck and shoulders and the way she tied her lovely blond hair with a big, bright ribbon behind her head. Depending on her mood, her blue eyes could sparkle with mischief or darken in mysterious thought. Her laughter was to me like the sound of the upper register of my automated church bells in Chicago's near north side, a series of liquid, cymbal-like sounds I shall never forget.

From the beginning, she wanted to be of service to both the church and to me. She quickly assumed the presidency of our Altar Guild, took responsibility for the junior grades of our church school, and even helped me with one or two articles in *Jesus Speaks*.

I had been impressed with her from the day I met her, the day I married her to Thomas Farrington beside a scrub oak on his large estate. Her attractiveness was enhanced by the very weather itself. It was one of those fresh, skin-tingling days only an island at sea can produce. Small, bright clouds scurried above us under the infinite blue of the sky. We could see and hear the surf as it thundered in—like God's words—from a leftover storm. The wind was spraying sheets of water and puffs of foam down the beach like recurring angels.

I had, of course, known Tom Farrington for years. He was not a member of my church or any other. I doubted, in fact, that he was or had ever been a Christian. But when he called me to tell me I would marry him—it was not a request—to his fourth wife, I could not refuse. One did not refuse Thomas Farrington with impunity.

Of course I had tried during many a summer month to win him to the Lord. That was before he became a full-time resident of our island. But in every interview I had with him, I found him a haughty and angry man. He had a way of thrusting out his jaw, chewing his tongue, and sniffing the air when he talked to you, as though he found every moment with you intolerable.

Barbara's first revelations to me of the indignities she suffered at his hands obviously reinforced these feelings. I wanted to intervene, find some way to shield her from the dark side of her husband's character. It was in my best interest—I should add in the best interest of my parish, as well—for me to believe there was a less-dark side to Thomas Farrington. After their marriage, the Farringtons became the largest contributors by far to our church programs. I attributed this generosity to Barbara's benign influence on that less-dark side of her husband's character.

But when I say indignities, I do not mean the usual domestic quarrels capped with a random beating. As terrible as those may be, such altercations happen relatively often on an island of hard-working laborers. Lobstermen, scallopers, cranberry boggers, carpenters: such men can spend long winter hours at rigorous manual tasks. These men may often suppress irresistible anger at their harsh and repetitive jobs and feel an overwhelming need for emotional release. I do not forgive their exuberances, their rages—I have felt such terrible needs myself—but I understand and try to deal with them in my own way, synonymous, I trust, with the Lord's.

But Tom Farrington's abuses were of quite a different magnitude. What right or need had he, a rich, retired businessman, a man of the world, to torture Barbara so? I was horrified and bitterly angry when I learned that he would sometimes fasten hideously painful clasps of his own design to her body, then pull at them until she fainted! And what right or need had he to tie her to a pole while his beastly dogs leapt around her, snarled and howled for the raw steak atop the pole? These were just a few of his abuses. There were others, more intimate, which Barbara was only able to reveal to me over time.

But I am getting ahead of my story. During one of her earliest talks with me, something like a divine revelation came upon me. I realized what God had been trying to tell me in the thunder of the surf and the flight of the angels that beautiful day I married Barbara and Tom. I saw in a flash, in an instant, God's plan for her.

Sitting on a mahogany chair in the rectory, she had been talking of an article for *Jesus Speaks*. Suddenly she said her husband was going mad. "Either that," she stammered, "or he is a terribly evil person." At those words, tears began rolling like great pearls down her pink, round cheeks. She seemed very uncomfortable, crossing and re-crossing her beautiful legs.

"I know I shouldn't say such things, Father. Fair is such a good man, really, down deep. But my life . . ." She broke down in sobs and for a while there was nothing more I could get from her.

I made some tea. As I think I've mentioned, there is nothing like tea with lemon and a bit of Sweet 'n Low to calm the nerves. In time she began the first of her confessions. It had to do with her allowance, the few dollars he gave her that were always conditional on his—she blushed enormously—satisfactions in bed or in other bizarre places of his choice. He kept a record of these—or the lack of them—in a small ledger beside the bed. With the frequency and extent of his satisfactions declining, her allowance had plummeted well beneath her needs. I should add that he had threatened, as well, to reduce or cut entirely their contributions to her various causes, including our church programs.

It was just about then that I had the revelation. Not an entirely shameless one, I freely admit. But it was irresistible and just. It would divinely resolve so many problems. With her unhappiness, her beauty, her wealth—albeit presently through her husband—and, above all, with her prayerful attitude toward our church and toward me, wouldn't

Barbara one day make a splendid wife and a perfect addition to my ministry? Together, what could we not achieve for the Lord? What great expectations could we not realize?

But back now to her bedroom and my adoring eyes upon her as she slept. Perhaps you can imagine with what contained excitement and sense of fulfillment I now viewed the future. With the passing of her husband—an event that had not been absent from my mind—so much might be achieved! Without shame or guilt, without looking back, I could now so freely contemplate the pleasures this very room and house would bring me. I thought of the house as my home, perhaps the new rectory. I thought of Barbara's assets as resources for an expanded budget, for building a new, more magnificent church, for attracting a much greater membership. I even dared to dream, just then, of expanding my ministry to the mainland and perhaps even the world! Yes, a ministry of love and devotion coming by radio and television to the whole world from "God's Little Island!"

I will not say that I had never before contemplated such wonders. While Thomas Farrington lived, I had put them out of my mind as fantasies bordering on un-Christian greed. But now? Now? As if to affirm my thoughts, her head slipped down on the pillow and she began snoring ever so peacefully.

Through the open window, I suddenly heard the sound of a motorcycle. Another interruption of my bliss! The damn machine roared around the circle, slid to a stop under my window. The doorbell rang, rang again. Whoever it was tried to force the door, then beat his fist against it.

Within half a minute I heard the maid arguing with him. His high-pitched voice sounded familiar to me. He had apparently pushed his way into the hall and seemed to be threatening her.

I opened our bedroom door. "Right now!" the shrill voice repeated. "Right now! I want to see her right now!"

Recognizing the voice, I closed the door and went downstairs.

At the sight of me, Budge Hill dropped his shrill tone. "Father? You? What are you doing. . . ?" He was silent for a moment, his eyes narrow, his thin lips quivering. When Budge concentrates, you can hear the machinery clanking. "Then it's true. You're here to . . ." His voice rose again. "The SOB is really dead! He bit it! He bit it!"

"You *idiot*!" I hissed. "Quiet down now!" I had never before–to his face, at least–called Budge an idiot. But the maid, possibly the cook, and–God help us–Barbara herself might have been listening. And how many times have I talked to Budge, in and out of jail, about his lack of judgement, his recklessness, to say nothing of his unruly temper and strength?

He blushed, looked down at the Oriental rug that ran the length of the hall. "I'm sorry, Father. I heard . . . There was a rumor in town that Farrington had died. I've been looking all over for you." He looked up, saw that the maid had gone back to the kitchen. A big smile disclosed his crooked teeth and a gold bridge. His shrill voice was back again. "The bastard bit it, Father! The bastard croaked!" His gloved fist was in the air, his eyes glittered.

I took the sleeve of his leather jacket and turned him toward the front door. Budge is six and one half feet tall. His frame is massive, his arms like the trunks of small trees. He has the physical power to do just about whatever he likes. But he followed me like a lamb through the door to the driveway.

My influence over him is partly that of priest over penitent. For years he has come to me for comfort, for good Christian advice and forgiveness. At heart he is a good man but seriously troubled by many demons.

One of these is his wife, Nettie, I believe. Though he says he loves her, he often complains of her control over him and her "bossiness." Especially irritating is her arbitrary allocation of family funds. Nothing is spent or purchased without her niggardly consent. In justice I should perhaps add here that I have never liked the woman. I find her profane and coarse. She gossips interminably, is sexually promiscuous. She has, I understand, a criminal record as well. But she is another story.

"Calm down, my son," I whispered, shutting the door behind me. "Control yourself. It is sinful to rejoice at death." I looked up at the bedroom window and whispered, "It is also a bit dangerous. The police believe, apparently, that there was foul play of some sort."

When Budge laughs his entire body trembles. His voice screeches like a subway train going around a sharp bend. "Foul play?" he screeched. "Foul play? Of course there was foul play!"

In his exuberance he bent down, put his arms around the Harley and lifted it as though it were a toy.

"Please, son," I whispered, "the widow is sleeping just above us here. Put that thing down!"

He threw the motorcycle down like one of his wrestling opponents. It bounced on its tires while he steadied it with one hand. "I came here to make sure it was true, Father. I wanted to know for sure that it was true."

Barbara, I knew, had befriended Budge. She was aware of my work with him, my attempts to strengthen his self-esteem. With my blessings, she had tried to discourage his wrestling and the unbridled fury that could erupt in the ring or in a bar. She was trying to interest him in books, reading to him, spending hours helping him to read.

"But where," I now asked Budge as he stood beside his motorcycle, "have you been, not to know the news? Tom Farrington died yesterday morning. The entire island is aware of it."

He winked at me, "Cruising this baby in Vermont. Dresser reunion." He looked up at Barbara's window, a big smile on his lips. He raised his gloved hands toward the window as though he'd just won a big match.

How much had Barbara told him of her trials with her husband? Why had he come out here when he'd first heard of Farrington's death? Had my secretary said I was here? Had he come to find me or Barbara?

I could ask him all that another day. Right now he needed to be warned against himself. When Budge Hill is in an ebullient mood, he can over-drink, turn boisterous and bitter, start fights. There is no holding him back.

"You'll stay away from the bars, won't you, son? You might say something you don't really mean and the police . . ."

To my surprise, he turned on me. "I'll say what I like! And fu . . . damn the police." An evil smile spread over his pale, fat face. "The Chief takes bribes. And more! He does things with little boys, too! Little boys. . . ? He's—"

His voice had risen, then cut right off. I stared at him in amazement. He lowered his head, ran the toe of his boot through the clamshells. "Sorry, Father. It's true, though. Takes bribes and does . . . things."

I reminded him, as I have so often before, that he must remember the work we had done together, our mutual prayers, especially the wonderful service of exorcism we had celebrated several years before. He had actually vomited out the Devil right there at the rail. I explained again that if he truly wanted Barbara and me to keep working with him, he must continue to keep the Devil out.

Budge wrapped his arms around me in a hug that forced my mouth and nose into his mud-stained leather jacket. As I was wondering how long it might take me to suffocate in such an embrace, he let me go. With both hands he lifted his giant leg over the seat of the Dresser. It whispered as it sank down under his weight.

"Dead," he said in much too loud a voice. "The SOB is really dead!" I saw another smile begin on his lips. He pressed the starter and squeaked out something I could not understand over the rumble of the engine. He took his hideous helmet from the handlebar of the bike, put it on quickly to cover his smile.

He would go to the Oven, a dingy, raucous bar. He would certainly get into trouble. There was nothing I could do to stop him. But I tried. "Remember," I shouted, "the meek shall . . ."

His engine roared, broken clamshells spewed behind the rear wheel. His only response was a big wave as he careened around the circle and headed for town.

CHAPTER FOUR

W hat Vado came back with, ten days later, was a warrant for my arrest. I didn't believe it! My worst nightmare come true.

Vado even pretended he was sorry to take me in. There were tears in his dark, beady eyes. "I . . . it's Horne, not me. I mean it don't add up, putting you in the slammer."

"Then what the fuck for?" I asked as calmly as I could.

Chick wiped his eyes with the back of his hand, put on his cop's voice. "You have the right to remain silent. Anything you say . . ." He paused. "I forget exactly . . ."

I knew there'd been rumors about Tommy's death. I'd even heard the police, maybe the FBI, were investigating it. I could feel sweat on the palms of my hands and I hardly ever sweat.

Vado had pulled a soiled piece of paper from his back pocket, was reading me the rest of the warning. "Nice going," I said when he'd finished. "You can actually read. But it doesn't mean a damn when you read it. Don't know your regulations, do you?"

His mouth opened for a second, his eyes wide. "Ah, c'mon," he whined, "cut it out, Hettie."

The Chief was waiting for us at the station. "Joey!" I said. "What the shit?"

He had a grim, defiant look on his face. We went into a little pink, windowless room, one big light bulb above the straight chair he gestured me to sit on.

"You need my help on this one, Chief?" Vado was leaning against the doorframe, hands in his pockets, casual. Like he was Philip Marlowe and not the little asslicker he always is around Joey.

The Chief nodded. "Take notes."

"Can he write?" I asked.

"No wisecracks!" Joey said. Chick came in and shut the door.

"Guess I'll need paper?" Chick said.

"Good Christ!" Joey whispered. "Maybe, just maybe, you can find some."

Chick opened the door and went out. "Now what's this all about?" I asked.

He just stared at me, grinding his teeth a little. "Joey!" I said. "It's me, Hettie. What the flaming fuck?"

"You're under arrest," he said, "for the murder of Thomas Farrington."

I don't remember exactly what I screamed at Joey but "asshole" was part of it. Which was a mistake, considering I have nothing against Joey's preferences.

He was grinding his teeth even harder, lips pulled back like Bogart before he kills somebody.

"I'm sorry," I said. "You're not really an asshole. And I'm not a murderer either."

"Don't speak," he said between his teeth, "until Vado gets back here."

"Ten to one he forgets a pencil," I said. I thought I saw a little smile at the corner of Joey's mouth. I looked around the room. "Nice pink," I said. "Becomes you, Joanie." It was what I called him in his formative years. It didn't work, of course. He just kept staring at me like we were meeting for the first time.

Chick came back and shut the door. He did have a pencil.

"I want a lawyer," I said.

"You'll get one," Joey said. "In the meantime, I have some questions."

"Makes two of us," I said.

"You ever hear of a heart stimulant called hexamillathonaroid?"

I shook my head but I had heard of it all right. The docs use it when they're giving injection stress tests to people who might have a heart attack if fully stressed out on the running machine. Makes the heart race like they were going full tilt.

"Where were you last night between midnight and three a.m.?"

"Sleeping," I answered, looking at Joey. "In my own little bed. What's it to you?"

"Did you know Silas Coffin was murdered last night?"

"Jesus!" I said.

"While he was performing an autopsy on Farrington's corpse," Joey said.

Chick decided to get in the act. "The killer locked Silas in one of his caskets. Silas suffocated while the killer went to work on Farrington's corpse. Broke him all up with a sledge hammer, chopped five fingers off his hands. Cut off his ears and his–"

"Enough!" Joey shouted. "I'm doing the questioning, if you don't mind."

I was thinking about those five fingers. But I said, "Silas was doing Farrington's autopsy last night? Farrington's been dead for ten days."

"Had to ice him, get a court order," Horne said.

"So I killed Farrington and Coffin?" I asked.

"No," Joey said. "Whoever killed Silas and dismembered Farrington was very powerful, huge, and careless. It obviously wasn't you."

"Don't underestimate me, Joey," I said. My armpits were soaking wet.

His next question was also a surprise. "Did you know Farrington was smuggling drugs?"

"You're out of your fucking mind," I whispered.

"Did you plan Farrington's or Coffin's death with anyone?"

"Shit no," I answered. "I'm a lot stronger than you think. And I'm a loner. Killed them both myself."

"I don't believe it!" Vado gasped, mouth open.

"Jesus," Joey and I said together. "Just write!" Joey said.

I'd been watching Chick. He hadn't so far written one damn thing on that pad. Now he was scribbling like mad. As though he'd been keeping the questions and answers in that moron head of his.

Joey ran his long, thin hands over his bald head. His nails were beautifully manicured. "Did you," he asked, "ever pick up any of Farrington's medicines and take them to his home?"

I knew I couldn't lie about that. Gretta Picket, our pharmacist, knew the truth. "Mrs. Farrington asked me to do that once or twice. I'd be on my way out to see her husband when he couldn't come to Island Life for his workout."

"What kind of medicines were they?"

"What am I?" I asked. "Some kind of doc or something?" I did know what they were, though: beta blockers, calcium channel blockers, nitros. Standard stuff for serious heart and arterial disease.

"You knew Farrington pretty well, didn't you?"

I nodded. "In some ways, I suppose."

"He held a mortgage on your club, didn't he?"

I nodded again. I thought of Vado's brain thinking how to write up a nod.

"Sorry, Chief. Do you spell mortgage with a 'j'?"

Joey just shook his head and continued with me. "Did you know you were in Farrington's will?"

"That's nice. For how much?"

"Did you know he forgave all his debts in his will?"

"What's that mean, exactly?"

"Did you . . . ah, did he ever force you to . . . have sex with him . . . in your sunroom, as you call it?"

"I want a lawyer," I said. I was feeling sick and I had to pee. "Could you turn that light down? It's fucking hot in—"

There was a hurried knock on the door. A voice said, "Rodney, Chief. Need you bad."

"Spit it out," Joey yelled.

"Er, kind of embarrassing, Joey."

"What isn't?" Joey shouted.

"Dickerson got into an argument with Elder and Elder has Dickerson's arms handcuffed around a cow."

"A *cow*? Jesus fucking Christ!" Joey said and left the room.

"Sam Elder!" I whispered to Vado. "He's your man, you little jerk!"

"My man?" Chick was still scribbling, but he stopped and looked at me. "My man?"

It didn't cover the hexamillathonaroid. It didn't cover Coffin or the smuggling, whatever that was about. But it sure covered the motive. And I could see from Horne's questions that I was going to need all the help I could get on motive.

I couldn't think of anyone on our island who wanted Tommy dead more than Sam Elder. Sam had worked on Tommy's new house. Tommy fired him and then published a full page ad in the *Mirror*. It said Sam was, among other things, the worst contractor in the state. The words, as I recalled later, were "a brain-damaged Cro-Magnon, unable to build a fire, much less a house."

Elder sued Tommy for libel, lost his case on the evidence of contractors and builders who'd seen Sam's sloppy work. Sam Elder told everyone Tommy had bought those witnesses and bribed the jury, all of which was probably true. But when Tommy sued Sam for defamation, Tommy won and Sam lost not only most of his money but all of his mind. All of his hair, too. He went around, half dressed, carrying an axe and swearing he'd chop Tommy into little pieces.

Vado glanced at the open door, whispered to me, "I shouldn't tell you this. But we looked into it, Sam I mean. He's been in the nuthouse for over a month. Just got out. Couldn't have been involved in this case."

"How could he have been in the nuthouse," I said, "if he wanted to kill a man like Farrington?"

Chick closed his mouth and nodded. "Hadn't thought of that. Adds up."

"Put her in number five," Joey said at the doorway. He was loading a clip into his gun.

"Number five?" I shouted. "I want my lawyer, Joey. Right now!"

"Let her call whoever she wants," Joey said, sticking his gun in his shoulder holster.

Vado cleared his throat. "I could continue the questioning, Chief. There's a lot on my mind. For instance, how could Sam Elder have been in the nuthouse if he wanted to kill a man like Farrington?"

Joey ground his teeth, reached for his handkerchief, and sneezed violently. "Don't open your mouth, you hear me? Let her call whoever she wants to call. Then put her in number five."

CHAPTER FIVE

I went to see Father Berry. It was the day after Hettie got out on bail. Rodney was keeping a tail on her and the Chief had asked me to talk to Father.

The priest had called the Chief to say he had some confidential information about Farrington and drugs. That meant the FBI or the Narcs. Which outfits, of course, Joey didn't want around. So Joey asked me to question Father on the credibility of his resources, their material-ness, hearsay, verify the . . . that sort of thing. It's complicated police and legal talk. You don't need to know all the nomen . . . nomen—all the rest of it.

I found Father sitting before a fire in his small house near the Heavenly Rest. That's his church, not a cemetery. He asked me to sit down but I told him I'd prefer to stand. A humungous brown cat with big testicles was prowling around my feet. I don't like cats at all. They know I don't like them and they very often leap into my lap when I'm sitting down. They try to get me to change my mind about them, that's how stupid they are. I sure didn't want this one on my lap. Those big testicles meant big claws and teeth. That's the way my mind went on it.

"I was expecting Chief Horne," Father said. He seemed upset. It sort of hurt my feelings.

"Sorry, Father. I'm on the Farrington case. The Chief's got the Coffin case."

"I thought they were one and the same," Father said. "Please sit down. Wasn't the Coffin killer trying to interfere with the Farrington autopsy?"

I rolled my eyes a little to indicate it was a complex question. The Chief, of course, is in charge of everything in our town. Naturally he has to relegate. But I didn't want to get into that.

Father said, "Chuck, isn't it?"

"Chuck's not involved," I said.

"No, no, your name's Chuck, isn't it?"

"No, it's not," I said. "But I'm doing the questioning, Father." And to be nice about it, I added, "If you don't mind."

"I don't mind at all," Father said crisply. "But could we stick to one subject or the other? You seem . . . disturbed."

I ground my teeth a bit like Joey does. Talk about hurt feelings! But a policeman keeps the upper hand. "Did you know Mr. Farrington's body was hacked to pieces by the Coffin killer?"

Father crossed himself. "Good Lord!" He sighed heavily.

I could see he was genuinely moved and I disliked asking him my next question. "With all due respect, Father, didn't you yourself tell me–threaten me, really–that an autopsy was a sin and God Our Father, not you, Father, might not protect me if I got involved with it?"

Father smiled, shifted his weight in the big chair. "You seem to have survived, so far. Now what do you want to know? And I insist, Chuck, for Heaven's sake, sit *down!*"

I thought about that for a moment. He could sure change the subject fast. But to humor him, I did sit down, leaning forward as far as possible. *No lap room for you, old cat,* was the way my mind went on it.

"Yes, let's get serious, Father. Apparently you told the Chief that Farrington might have been smuggling drugs. That's a serious charge, isn't it? Especially when the charged person will have difficulty defending himself?" At the word "difficulty," I laughed a bit. You know, just in order to keep the conversation lighthearted.

Father didn't smile and I made a mental note of that. "I thought it might help your investigation," Father said. "Mrs. Farrington is my source, if that's what you're interested in knowing."

I pulled out a sheet of paper. The Chief hadn't thought too much of my not having paper when he was questioning Hettie. "Mind if I take a note or two, Father?"

"Perhaps the Chief would prefer to talk directly to Mrs. Farrington about this. She's feeling considerably better."

"Really?" I said. "Her husband's dead less than three weeks and now she's better? Adds up, you think?" I shot a significant glance at him. Maybe the cat didn't like that glance. I felt the claws of its big paw through my trousers.

"Are you all right, Chuck? Stomach upset or something?"

"That's interesting, Father. Why would you say something like that?"

"You just said ouch. And your position. You're leaning. . . ?"

"Forward," I said, observing what he was observing. "I'm very interested in this case, Father. A good friend of mine may be in some serious trouble. No, I'm sorry, strike that, Father. I shouldn't have mentioned it, but it's a little heavy on my heart. Please go back to what you were saying about . . ." I looked down at my notes but I hadn't taken any yet.

"I was talking about Mrs. Farrington," Father said. "She is a woman of the Lord. Together we are helping her overcome her grief and go forward. She's very anxious, of course, for the interment."

"Oh we'll get him, Father. Be interr, whatever, for a long, long time. Life maybe. I don't believe in the death penalty, but it's a matter of opinion, really."

The good man sighed again. He seemed tired. He sat with his hands folded in his lap, his legs crossed. I couldn't figure why he was so dressed up: turned white collar, light gray suit with a vest and pocket watch. He probably wore garters to hold up his socks, but I really don't know why I thought of that. Maybe I shouldn't have. I let out one heck of a shout. Father Berry and I were on our feet while the cat clung to my shoulder and the top of my head like a demon from hell.

"*Augustine*!" Father yelled. He took the cat in his hands, removed it from my shoulder. The top of my head hurt where the demon's claws had probably pierced the skin. "Outrageous!" Father said to the beast. "Sorry, Chuck. I've never seen him do that before. Unforgivable!"

"It's all right," I whispered. "In my line of work . . . prepared for everything. Just about."

We sat down again and I tried to remember where we were. "Could you tell me what Mrs. Farrington told you, I mean about the smuggling?"

He answered my question at length, as they say. I'm afraid I can't give you word for word what he said. I had a pencil with me but the lead was broken off.

In general, it was this way. Farrington was always very cruel to his wife. One of the terrible things he did was to force her to help him when certain supplies were delivered from a boat off shore. It was usually in the winter, about three a.m., windy and freezing cold.

Together they'd roll the crane down its track, lower his speedboat into the ocean. Then, while she shivered and shook on the beach, he'd drive out to the boat. It might even have been a submarine. She could never see it in the dark. Just a bobbing light or two out pretty far.

Of course I was appalled. Can you imagine that? Letting a woman freeze like that on a cold beach?

Sometimes he was gone one hour, sometimes two or three. Usually he came back drunk and with boxes and bags marked *Gracious Homes*. He called them home improvements. She'd help him get the boat out of the water, roll the crane back, carry the bags and boxes to a locked and secret cellar under the house.

Of course I asked Father Berry what Farrington did with the bags and boxes. I mean were there a lot of improvements on his house?

Father shook his head. There were *obviously*–I notice he emphasized that word–never any improvements made from the things in the cellar. Just what Farrington did do with the bags and boxes was not clear. Mrs. Farrington hadn't gone into that. He imagined they were flown off by helicopter or simply taken over by truck on the ferry.

"Couldn't have been drugs, then," I told him. "Much too dangerous. He'd have been nuts. Ah!" I laughed. "Dope on the ferry? Ha ha!"

Father frowned and went on about the deceased's miserable treatment of his wife. It was shocking to me because I never understand cruelty to womanhood. It seems that the "brute," as Father called Farrington, made his wife sniff–the precise word Father used was "snort"– the contents of one of the bags the brute had brought in from the sub. She liked the feeling it gave her and it seems she became attached to the contents of that particular bag, though she never knew what it was.

Here Father put his hand over his eyes and I remember what he said. "She would go down on her knees to beg him for it. It helped her with," Father actually sobbed right then, "some of the terrible things he forced her to do."

"What a brute," I said. "I'm beginning to understand this case a lot better, Father."

He had stopped sobbing. "Congratulations!" he said.

I wasn't certain I liked his tone of voice. It sounded a bit mean. Maybe I shouldn't have accused him of threatening me about the autopsy. Some people can be upset by threats, remember them, too.

In my business, though, you can't risk looking back at your mistakes. Besides, it sounded as though there really was a drug angle to Father's story and Joey would be darned interested in that.

My mind was working fast. If Farrington was moving drugs to the mainland, he was probably mixed up with the Mafia. If the Mafia was in it, they were using Farrington one way or the other. Probably for big stakes, big money. If they were playing for big money and if Farrington knew too much or hadn't played their game, bang! End of Farrington.

The problem was they didn't bang him. He died of a heart attack. Sure, pushed along by that medicine and by Hettie who maybe unintentionally got him worked up. But heart attack nonetheless. And the Mafia don't work that way. It's bang! and you're out!

"Bang?" Father asked.

"Just doing a little analysis," I said.

"Congratulations!" Father said.

It was beginning to annoy me, that word. Of course, I knew he was feeling very sorry for Mrs. Farrington and meant well enough. But it seemed a bit mean, really.

I needed time to finish my analysis before I left off questioning. "Mrs. Farrington sounds like a very interesting person. Could you tell me something about her, Father? You know, her family backdrop, her education, that sort of thing. Nothing personal, of course. Just off the record. I don't plan to write it down or anything like that."

While he was going on about Barbara Farrington–how charming she was, how intelligent, her wonderful education, her marriage, how much she'd suffered in the past–I tried to get my thoughts together. My head hurt and I was expecting the cat, still roaming around my legs, to make another leap at any moment. I felt the top of my head and, sure enough, there was a little wet spot where a claw had gone in. I decided right then and there that as soon as I left Father's house, I would drive to the emergency room of the hospital for a shot of antibiotic or whatever the doc on duty thought was necessary, like a rabies injection or something. I wasn't going to get knocked off this case by a cat with big testicles, no matter how mean it was.

"As a matter of fact," Father was winding up his praises of Barbara Farrington, "I'm going to see her for lunch this afternoon. Since the death of her husband, she's contemplated some various services for the church and me. I'm very excited about that."

So that was why he was so dressed up! He was making a parish call and wanted to impress her. I wondered what they'd be having for lunch. I was getting that hungry, in spite of the pain on the top of my head.

"Well, enough," I said rising from my chair. "You've been very open with me, Father." I pretended to study the room. "Just a final question." I threw a sharp, meaningful look at him. "Has it occurred to you that the Mafia–you know, the Italians–might have something to do with this?" He looked startled and I laughed engagingly. "Careful now, I warn you, I'm Italian. Real name is Chinkway, means five in Italian."

He stood up to shake my hand. "So that's why they call you Chuck, eh? Incidentally, it's very bright of you to conjecture that Tom Farrington might have been working with the Mafia. That's an Italian organization, eh?"

I had a feeling he was hiding something. There was a little smile on his lips. I made a note to make a note of that smile. Very curious.

Then he said something I didn't like. "I hope your Chief and other qualified authorities will talk with Mrs. Farrington about all this." I don't know why, but it hurt my feelings, you know. Qualified authorities?

So our talk didn't end very well. "Don't let the cat out," he said as I opened the front door. But it was too late. The last words I heard him say were "God almighty!" Which hurt, too. All things considered, it wasn't my best day.

CHAPTER SIX

Barbara Farrington's oversized bed was the most luxurious I have been privileged to share. Blue satin sheets, large down pillows, cashmere blankets are covered, when it is made up, with a satin quilt and a colorful variety of three-and four-cornered throw pillows. The bed, at the moment, was quite definitely not made up.

"Bobbie," as I had begun to call her, was lying on her back, one arm thrown over her head. From the abandoned position of that arm and the faint smile on her lips, I was initially certain she had indeed undergone what I call the Visitation. By it, I mean that climactic feeling, during sexual intercourse, of the presence of the Holy Ghost.

The idea of such an experience is unfortunately not original with me. I say unfortunately because it is a true, splendid, and often useful concept. Its origins can be found—as I frankly admit in my special sermon on the subject—in T. Pettibone and Roger Gomper's classic works. They describe at some length the marvelous orgasmic nature of Jesus that so awed and outraged the Jews and the Romans. I refer you to the text of my sermon, published in *The American Christian* on May 22, 1984, for further information on the origins and history of the concept.

Needless to say, it has served my ministry well and caught the rapt attention of many of my current and former parishioners.

So far as Bobbie and I were just now concerned, I readily admit that my own Visitation had so enthralled me as to make impossible the monitoring of hers. This was due, in part, to past successes. I tend—it is not entirely a Christian value—to take for granted the gratifications my ministry customarily affords.

With Barbara Farrington, a few doubts had begun to cloud my mind. I have stressed that she was quite different from the other women of this island. I was speaking then of her appearance and character prior to the death of her husband. In the weeks following it, these differences had taken a somewhat darker turn. She seemed, in her days of mourning, an unsettled mixture of compassion and reserve, of tenderness and distraction. There was in her manner a distance, a daze, a coolness I was not certain the Lord or I could ever entirely overcome.

For example, there was a certain indifference in the way her naked body was now stretched out on the blue sheet. Her face had its customary beauty and innocence. But her body said something else. Her breasts hung back under her armpits, her knees were up and spread in almost wanton abandonment.

Was I oversensitive? How many women after Visitation wouldn't have covered their naked bodies with a sheet? Or portions of it with pillows or a modestly placed hand? I could not help but wonder whether this apparent lewdness indicated some deficiency of character. Or was it merely the result of an insufficient Visitation?

Her conversation sometimes seemed inappropriate, as well. This was our second holy coupling. Does one talk, after such an experience, of one's former relationships? "And I must," she was saying, "tell you a secret. For all of Fair's insults and abuse, I truly loved him. His misfortunes and dilemmas were never understood, really. Except by me, by me." Here she scratched her foot, pulling one knee up to her chin. Her exposure was complete and made me, just then, quite uncomfortable.

Yet I couldn't object to it. My relationship with Barbara was proceeding more rapidly than I'd anticipated. I was pleased, of course. But it was much too soon to criticize her. Everything was going too well to risk that right now. I told myself that the good Lord had constructed us as we are. What shame is there in nudity of any kind?

I, too, was naked, turned on my side, my head supported by my bent arm. While for the moment she was silent, enjoying her scratching, I could not resist asking an important question. "That story about your husband's drug smuggling. I discussed it, as you asked me to, with one of Horne's deputies this afternoon. May I ask whether the story was entirely true?"

She laughed and reached for the "Chalice," as I call it, still quite moist from our encounter. "You do ask the silliest questions, Ralphie." She shook it in time with her words, "The sill . . . sill . . . silliest quest . . . quest . . . questions!"

I reached to stop her hand which was causing a mild bit of pain. "No, truly," I said, "I do want to know the truth. And I forgive you, if you were forced to lie. Forgiveness is one of our more glorious principles. The Church would be elsewhere without it."

"It's a long, sad story," she sighed. "You see, Fair was in the grip of evil men." She squeezed at the word "grip." "The dreadful grip, do you understand, the terrible, terrible grip of greed!"

I nodded and again tried gently to remove her hand. She clung desperately to the Chalice as though she wanted more fully to understand its mysteries. "Fair was, you know, in the clothespin business. He invented all sorts of new pins, clasps, and fasteners. One of them—it looked more like the jawbone of a large animal—could clasp and hold almost any object, no matter its form or weight.

"It was his favorite invention. He invested huge amounts of his own money in its development and manufacture. Unfortunately there was very little market for it. It didn't sell. And during his second marriage, poor thing, he was forced into bankruptcy."

Bobbie took her hand away to adjust her pearl necklace, which had worked under her back. A small segment of it clung tightly to her neck like—I could not avoid the analogy—a noose or garrote. Was this some sort of subconscious reference to her husband's death . . . or, God help me, to hers?

She laughed bitterly, told me that Marion, his second wife, had left him, taking both of their children. Marion had thought they'd all be going to the poorhouse. She had, she made clear, more attractive options.

Bobbie sat up, put a pillow behind her head and caressed the long string of pearls down between her breasts to her silken hair. She had, for a woman in her forties, a remarkable, Reubenesque figure. In spite of my distaste for Reubens, I was stirred by her coarse movements and realized another Visitation might well be upon us.

"What happened," she continued, "was that several sleazy investors staked Fair to a new corporation with enough capital to buy up most of the clothespin competitors both here and abroad. They took, of course, a very large share of the equity. But with Fair's share and his remarkable management, he became in time quite rich.

"At the beginning he had no idea his investors were the Mob, a particularly powerful branch of it. They were, as it turned out, laundering drug money, great quantities of it.

"I met Fair during his third marriage. Bridgett was a little cunt, if you'll excuse the expression. She was screwing several of the investors, spending Fair's money on luxury cruises to Sicily and heaven knows where else. Nobody liked her very much, and Fair decided she'd taken one too many cruises and, ah, suggested they make sure her travels were really over.

"By this time his company had gone public. He was a multimillionaire. But with the money laundering and his helping Bridgett to—would you say heaven, Ralphie darling?—he was by then totally their creature. They forced him to purchase this land and build this house. Their goal was to use it and him for the smuggling I told you about."

She breathed in deeply, the mound of her wrinkled belly rising gently. She raised her leg again, this time to scratch a cheek, her exposure as complete as before. In spite of her immodesty and insensitivity, the Chalice had grown to its more sacred size. "Goodness!" she said when her hand reached for it again. "Is the Holy Ghost getting its second wind?"

I do not respect such blasphemous language, and my face must have told her so. "Oh, Ralphie dearest. You know how I worship the Lord and the spirit that moves him."

I took her in my arms and both of us—I'm eighty percent sure about her—were blessed with such a supreme Visitation I was forced to take a nitro-glycerin for my angina.

Afterwards, when she had come back to bed, her eyes a bit glazed, she was wearing— I'm pleased to say—a negligee of sorts. She wanted me to tell her in detail what had happened in my interview with the deputy policeman. And why hadn't the Chief been there? "I was," she said petulantly, "trying to learn what we could by telling them about the beach events and the drugs. My lawyers would be furious with me for telling you about that."

"Lawyers?" I asked. "You have lawyers? More than one?"

She smiled. "Any number I want. But there is one, very cute too, who would be the most angry. So we won't tell him, will we, darling Ralphie? Now go on, tell me what you learned. Who do they suspect?"

I explained that if the police suspected anyone, I would not have learned it from the idiot who came to talk to me in the Chief's place. I had seriously doubted whether he could spell his own name.

Barbara was angry for a moment. I could see the fire in her eyes. "Why didn't you refuse to talk to the man? Call the Chief himself? All you men are so . . . never mind!"

She began then to arrange a number of those throw pillows around and in back of her so that she could sit up and smoke a cigarette. I'm quite against smoking—a dirty, dreadful habit of the Devil. But this was not, as I've said, the time for criticism. Instead, I told her, by way of the strangest, most ridiculous news in our island *Mirror*—our weekly newspaper—that one of our policemen had been handcuffed to a cow's neck. The officer's arms were too short to pass over the cow's head, the animal had panicked and broken both of the officer's feet.

Barbara screeched with laughter. "I'll bet it was that Vado fellow, the one who's afraid of my weimeraners!"

I told her I thought the wiremonger fellow was the one who had interviewed me this morning. "Horne," I suggested, "must hire them for something other than their brains. In fact, there's a rumor Horne has some very odd sexual preferences." I crossed myself but couldn't help smiling. "God help me for spreading such a rumor."

She laughed, spread her negligee open and brought her knees up. I'm pleased to say that the ashtray atop a scarlet pillow on her lap did not spill its contents on either of us.

She had not, of course, bothered to brush her dyed blond hair. It hung in tangles. With the cigarette dangling from her mouth, she had again that debauched look. I had not realized the extent of the civilizing effort I would have to make in the Lord's plan for her. Unless . . . some such trouble as had ended her husband's life should . . . But it was much better, just then, not to think too far into the future. There was much to be accomplished in the present.

She drew enormously on her cigarette. "Tell me whether your idiot of this morning told you anything about the autopsy. What have they found?"

Isolated and in mourning here at North Point, she had not heard of Silas Coffin's death or the unexpected desecration of her husband's body. I did not relish telling her that but, sitting up and covering the Chalice, I did my best. "I'm afraid," I said, "that there is some bad news about that."

She blew a long stream of smoke in my face. I coughed. "Sorry," she said. "What bad news?"

"An intruder, a maniac, suffocated the coroner while he was . . . ah, examining your husband. Whoever it was wanted, apparently, to stop the autopsy."

"And. . . ?"

I decided to spare her the bits and pieces. "Enough work had been done prior to Silas's death, enough communicated to the police, for them to know that Thomas had taken hexamillathonaroid the morning of his death."

Barbara stubbed out her cigarette. "I don't believe it! Is that some kind of poison?" She put her head in her hands. "I never thought Fair would try to kill himself."

"They don't think that at all," I said. Then I told her about the substitution of medicines in his heart capsules and the physical stress that had killed her husband.

She looked up at me with tears in her eyes. "Poor Fair, oh poor dear Fair."

I was instantly annoyed. "Your late husband was cruel to you, a beastly, godless man! You must, as I've said many times, try to put him out of your mind, well away from you."

She kissed me then, very quickly on the cheek. "You've helped me so, putting him away from my mind, I mean. I do want it all to really end, though. Have they any idea who could have. . . ?"

"They've arrested a woman named Hill. You don't know her. An immoral—"

"Hettie Hill. The owner of Island Life! I know her. She was Fair's trainer. She came to this house from time to time to work with him."

"The police," I said softly, "believe she worked him a little too hard." It was what the town was talking about and Barbara had seen the body at Island Life. But she didn't laugh. She thought about it for a moment, then fumbled for the Chalice under the sheet. "The name of that medicine or whatever it is that they found in Fair's body? What is it? How do you know about it, the strange name and all?"

It was a question I did not want to answer fully. "I have parishioners," I replied. "You needn't concern yourself with how I know things. Some of my people are in high places."

She pulled at the Chalice. "Please, Ralphie, I know about Jesus and other high places of yours." She gave it another pull. "Tell me who told you, please."

I told her that as a priest I had sworn to keep certain confidences. She insisted, moved near me, her fingers squeezing the sacred sack the Chalice lay upon. "What do I have to do, dear, to have all your confidences?"

I could think of several things, one for which a Chalice is used. But I would save that for another time; the Ghost had made its presence known for today. "All right," I said, removing her hand. "There is a woman I've attended in the past. She's the wife of Samuel Elder, who has been in a sanitarium for many weeks. She's employed by the police department as dispatcher and secretary. Knowing how much all this meant to you, dearest, I asked Marsha Elder for information. She was quite pleased to give it to me."

Barbara's face was suddenly frightened. "It's the maid," she whispered, "coming home earlier than I expected. We'd better get dressed, darling. She'll be up here in two shakes of a lamb's tail." Perhaps I need not add that she then gave two little shakes to . . . yes, of course you've guessed it.

CHAPTER SEVEN

Wade Waters Wade convinced Judge Adolph Hoguet I wouldn't run to Mexico. That and a one hundred thousand dollar bail bond–paid for with a chunk of my Island Life savings–got me out of the slammer. Two fucking nights I was in there and all Wade Waters Wade had to say when we said goodbye at the courthouse was, "See you back here soon, Hettie. Real soon!"

Three W, as we call him, is a rich Summer Tanner turned rich island lawyer. Like everyone else in his profession, he's an asshole: shameless, up-tight, arrogant. But I know him from when we were kids, me cutting lawns and washing windows, him playing croquet and watching me washing windows. We dated once, just once. When he tried to kiss me, grabbing my ass in his fat, flabby hands, I kneed him so hard he puked in the sand. Poor Wadie. I'll bet his cock was blue for a month.

I felt real bad about that, apologized, washed his mom's windows for free once in a while. Believe it or not, we stayed friends. And after he gave up his practice in New York City and moved here, I asked him to handle all the legal shit to get Island Life going.

Three W was the lawyer who drew up my mortgage note to

Tommy Farrington. That's right, the note that motivated me to kill Tommy, according to Joey Horne, the prick! Of course that was only one of my reasons for killing him. I was in Tommy's will for two hundred and fifty thousand dollars. I hated him, too, because he forced me to blow him in the sunroom. They were right about most of those motives. But I'll tell you this. Tommy wanted me to blow him but, so help me God, I never did it. Made me sick to even think of doing it, I hated him that much.

So, according to Joey Horne, I picked up Tommy's medicine, substituted a poison—call it a heart breaker—for the medicine, worked him into cardiac arrest on the lat-pull. And now they were charging me with everything from conspiracy and manslaughter to first degree murder. They were both right and wrong.

Anyway, I was in a whole shitload of trouble. All I had to do now was wait for them to get their case in order, be tried here or on the mainland, be convicted, then shoved into prison again, this time for life. Unless I could find an alibi, give them another theory, find some other suspect.

Of course I could get my little ass off the island, get lost in South America or some place. But I like it here! It's got advantages you don't have in South America, like stupid cops and haughty-ass Summer Tanners, out-of-sight rentals, over-priced groceries, traffic tie-ups, horny priests. But why was I trying to be funny? I was scared shitless and had only a few days of freedom to get myself out of the mess I'd made for myself.

There were hundreds who might have wanted Tommy dead. But there were only a few, in addition to me, who would have had something real personal to gain from killing him. Unless I could show that he'd gotten on the wrong side of someone he was smuggling for. Why had Joey mentioned that? Maybe to help me? But I couldn't run around looking for unknown smugglers. All I could really do was go after those who appeared to be good suspects. I'd drawn up a long list of three. And Father Ralph Berry was at the top of it.

First I had to clear up a real frightening problem. That's right, those five fingers cut off Tommy's dead body. I've told you about me and fives. Were the five missing fingers a coincidence or were they cut off to implicate me? Or were they chopped off out of spite by some incredibly strong, stupid jerk? Who knew about my fives? That was my first project.

My house was a mess, coal stove out, dirty dishes in the sink, not the usual signs or sounds of Budgy. I wouldn't have known he was in the bathtub except for a sock just outside the bathroom door.

His black leather jacket and trousers were under one boot on the bathroom floor. His jockeys and undershirt were in the sink. With the other boot still on his foot, he was curled up in the bathtub or maybe I should say on the bathtub. One leg and one arm were dangling down over the side. His head hung over the end of it.

I don't think I ever loved him more. He was so naked and helpless, lying there, snoring, breathing in and out like an exhausted rhinoceros. Ordinarily, I would have let him sleep. But today was different.

When I turned the cold shower on, he let out a high-pitched scream—he has a beautiful tenor voice. Grunting and screaming, he tried to get his feet under him. When he did, slipping and teetering, he rose like a sea monster, water radiating from him and spraying the bathroom. He stood there a moment, shivering and shaking like in a fit, those beautiful brown eyes of his bulging and out of focus.

I turned off the shower, got up on the toilet seat to dry his head. He was gasping for breath as my towel went over his nose and mouth.

"Got to talk to you, baby. Things are bad, very bad!"

His voice shook. "I didn't qualify. . . ? For Macho Man Randy. . . ?"

"Not that," I said, stepping down from the toilet. I dried his big, hairless chest, his belly and his shriveled little pecker and balls. He looked down at me suspiciously.

"What'd I do wrong?"

God how I love him when he's like that, a little boy whose hand's been in the cookie jar.

He stepped out of the tub and I dried his back and buns. They're like round boulders. Real cute.

"Where you been, Het?"

"Slammer," I said, working on the backs of his legs, hairy and elephant thick.

He turned. "What's that?"

"I know. I should have called you. But I thought you were in Burlington or someplace. They gave me one call only, to Three W. He got me out of there just now."

My Budge was so upset he squeaked. "But how . . . why were they. . . ?"

I put my face against his chest and fondled his pecker. "I love you, honey, and I know you love me. It'll be all right."

He put his hand over my head and pressed it hard against his chest. "But I . . ."

"I'll tell you everything," I said, still working on his pecker which was growing in my hand. "But first I have some questions for you. Unless you'd rather we took a little trot before that?"

"Umm," he murmured, pressing his pelvis forward. Budgy's erections are not huge. I mean, he isn't built like an elephant everywhere. When it's hard, it's more like a thick steel bolt, short and sharp. It can hurt if you're not careful. It was like that now and, in spite of the delay, just what I wanted.

You see, Budgy has a tendency to lie, to tell things in the way he thinks you'd like to hear them. I've found over the years that the best time to get him to tell the truth is when we're trotting—that's our word for fucking.

I guess we use that word because that's more or less the way we have to do it, trotting I mean. With Budgy, any position other than my being on top, side saddle, or astride, is very risky. Some part of me is sure to get broke if he's on top or even beside me. Ribs, pelvis, you name it!

All that has happened before. Once, in our early days, he cracked my nose and almost suffocated me under that chest of his. Sometimes, when he's not in training, he weighs as much as 310 pounds, can you believe it?

Anyhow, I'm safer on top. I ride him out, posting when necessary. But the point of telling you this is to say there are moments, just before he breaks into a gallop, when he can't lie to me. "Yes or no, I say, rising up a bit, are you trotting with Mrs. X?" Or, "Did you put all your prize money in our account?" And by God, he tells me the truth, even about his little girl fans, though I don't ask him about them anymore. They really mean nothing to him.

The problem with Budgy is married women. Early on I caught him in a lie. It was about fucking with Mrs. Y, let's call her. When I found out the truth, I told him he'd lied to me and I was cutting off his allowance and his trotting for six months. Sure, I told him, I was pissed about Mrs. Y. But he wouldn't have been broke and trotless for anything like six months, if he'd told the truth. As far as I know, he never lied to me after that.

This time what I had to ask him was the most important question of my life. It could lead me to my alibi. Maybe you can guess what it was. I always thought Budgy was the only person who knew my fear of fives, about my going to prison for five years on the fifth day of the fifth month and the other stuff. But maybe Budgy had told someone else about my fives and that someone had killed Silas and broken Tommy up like that to point the five fingers at me. Maybe Joey didn't know about that yet. But maybe the person Budgy told was my number one alibi. I had to know.

Or then again, maybe Budgy himself had cut off those fingers? I didn't believe that. He wouldn't have given a damn about the autopsy. And besides, he was a high school and drinking buddy of Silas Coffin. But when Budgy drinks, he can go a little wild. I was real scared he got stinking drunk, broke into the freezer, and cut off the fingers of the dead man while Silas was out of his office or on vacation.

Why would he do that? Because he hated Tommy like everyone else. Maybe he'd heard rumors about Tommy and me in the sunroom and wanted to get back at Tommy for that. All this was pretty crazy. The cops had the idea one person killed Silas and then broke Tommy up. They're morons but they probably thought they had some good evidence for that. Mostly it didn't make sense for Budgy to do such a nutty thing. I mean, to implicate me with or without intention. I had to know the truth.

So that's a long way of telling you why I was now on Budgy who was wheezing and groaning at a fast trot. Astride in the saddle, I was enjoying myself but watching for the best moment to catch the truth from him. When he goes into a gallop or a run, he's speechless and I'm too late. Naturally, I was urging him on. As I say, this was a fucking important trot we were doing.

"Yeah, baby! Go boy!" I whispered, sitting it out, but posting now and then, which he likes.

I saw his eyes start to roll. So I rose up just enough above the bolt to drive him crazy. "Did you take five fingers off Farrington's dead body, yes or no?"

He looked up at me in amazement. I lowered my body just a little, raised it again. "Yes or no, baby. Tell Momma the truth."

He shook his head, his eyes wild with desire.

"Yes or no, my baby!"

"No, no!" he squeaked.

"That's my little boy. Now one more question. Did you ever tell your favorite priest, Father Berry, about my fear of fives?" I gave him a deep one and slowly raised up again. "The truth. Give it to me, honey! Momma wants the truth to save her ass!"

Budgy was staring at me as though I'd lost my mind. He suddenly bucked up to get going again. I was too quick for him and he squealed, "Yes! Yes! I told him, I told him!"

I smiled and he reached those ham hands of his around my waist and shoved my ass down on him with a whack you could have heard on the mainland. He gave a great war whoop, galloped, ran. Still running, he suddenly bucked me up in the air. I've never seen him do it quite like that. He took his hands off my waist and bucked me so hard I went up two feet, came down, thank God, in a good fit. Then once more up and down. And that time he let out that long shriek of his I always wait for, that always makes me happy for him.

Doubly happy today because I knew now just where I was going next. He was my baby, though. So after I stopped kissing him and before I left the house, I made him his favorite dinner: macaroni and cheese, baby limas, mashed potatoes out of a box, and chocolate ice cream with chocolate sauce.

I should have stayed home. Maybe I was just too happy at what Budgy'd told me. Father and the fives and all. Maybe it was the trotting and bucking. I don't know. I got careless, that's for sure.

And things went fucking bad.

I knew Father Berry wasn't at home. I telephoned his house while I was heating that sauce for Budgy. There was no answer and it was the fifth time I'd tried him. I didn't think of that until later!

When I got into my car, I saw Rodney standing by a battered truck across the street. He was disguised, dressed in a clamming outfit, waders and all. He even had a clam rake and a big barrel in the back of the truck. He was also wearing a handle-bar mustache with a Harpo Marx wig under a Red Sox baseball cap.

Rodney is a cop, the fourth of a full-time force of four. Not five, thank God! Rodney's even dumber than Chick Vado, which almost isn't possible.

He'd been following me, for sure. I wondered how much he'd heard when I and Budge were at it. I smiled, thinking of him standing at our bedroom window in that clamming outfit, listening to Budgy whooping. What a show, if he'd been there. Which I doubted. He'd be afraid to come too close to the house.

Even if he had, I'd whispered the words "Father Berry." So he sure didn't know where I was heading. But I had to lose him and it wasn't that difficult.

I drove slowly, parked at Island Life. When I went in, I whispered to Jo Ellen who's always in her sweats. I changed into her street clothes, put a towel over my head, went back out and got into her car. Driving away, I could see the mustached clammer peeking through the downstairs window at the sexy little Summer Tanners doing aerobics.

Father Berry's is where I got stupid. I just rang the bell a couple of times and walked in. His cat, a big, beautiful Siamese, mewed around me. I picked him up and began searching the house.

What I wanted to find was evidence, any evidence, that Ralph Patrick Berry had murdered Thomas Farrington. He was the only suspect on my list who had the education and the brains to figure such a complicated, suspicion-free way to kill a man with a heart disease.

And no one had a better motive to kill Tommy than a horny priest who needed money and a wife. I know, Episcopal priests run away with their parishioners almost every week. The churches are full of such pricks. Find the right believer, fuck her, forgive her, run away with her. So what else is new? You just usually don't have to kill the husband. Unless he's got all the money. And this husband did.

After searching the rooms downstairs, I put the cat down and went upstairs. It was dark and silent and smelled like a funeral home. I went into the bathroom at the top of the stairs, shut the door and pulled out the top drawer of an old chest. I went through Father Berry's medicines and personal effects for five or six minutes.

I had just gotten to a stack of his condoms when I heard a horrible noise. It came from Father Berry's bedroom next to the bathroom. It was the long, drawn-out scream of a cat being tortured or dying. I know what cats sound like when they're hurt.

I should have taken off right then. The bedroom door was closed and maybe, if there was someone in there with the cat, he hadn't heard me. But I love cats and there was a real hurt cat in that room!

I knocked on the door. "Anybody in there?" I whispered. No answer. I knocked louder. "Hello?"

The door opened fast and a big guy stood there. He was dressed in a dark, pinstriped suit and vest, white button-down shirt, yellow bow tie, and a black fedora. He had a brown stocking stretched down tight over his head and face.

He just stared at me for a moment, didn't say a word. Then he slowly turned and gestured toward the bed. The Siamese was lying on Father Berry's quilt, blood pumping from its neck. It didn't have a head.

The hooded man held his big hairy hand out to me. The cat's head was in his palm. Its green eyes stared at me, its pink mouth open, its white teeth bared. I thought I was going to throw up. They tell me I fainted, instead.

CHAPTER EIGHT

Of course we had to put Hettie in the slammer again. Violation of bail bond, breaking and entering, suspicion of cruelty to animals. But I'll go back to the beginning—well, sort of the beginning.

You see, I'd answered Father's 911 and found Hettie unconscious in the upstairs hall. I also found a cat without a head laying in a pool of blood on Father's double bed. Is it "laying" or "lying"? I never get it right. And my mom's voice keeps telling me I'm wrong. Irregardless— I do remember that one—you don't get many 911s about cats with no heads.

Father later said he'd thought Hettie was dead, saw the cat's bloody body, and ran from the house in fear for his life. I guess he had good reason. The town doc who saw the dead cat said its head had been ripped off its body. The neck bone and the wind pipe were that twisted and stretched. It would have taken, he said, incredible dexterity and strength. Gives me the creeps.

But you have to be prepared for all kinds of things in my business, know how to take advantage of strange circumstances. For example, I suggested to Joey we should start a search for the cat's head. Call people to check their trash cans, that sort of thing. Search Mount Trashmore, that's what we call our dump.

Hettie had said she saw the head in Yellow Tie's hand. That's what we were calling the intruder she talked about. In police work you have to shorten your descriptions of suspects, even when you're not sure they are suspects. We were, I should add for the record, a little doubtful about Hettie's story of Yellow Tie. I mean, where was the head, for heaven's sake? That was just the point. If we found the head, we would know more about Yellow Tie and his habits. Joey said "Screw it!" to the idea. But he's not always as smart as some people say.

Wade Waters Wade tried to spring Hettie but this time without success. Still, he's a genius, and he's taking her case even with all the evidence we have against her. If I ever need a lawyer, Three W is going to be my man. For Hettie, he was even willing to put up the bail bond money. He tried to convince Judge Hoguet that Hettie went to Father Berry's for religious counseling and advice. I wasn't too sure of that myself. Hettie wasn't at all religious, though I've heard that her husband, Budgy, went to Father Berry for counseling. Believe me, Budgy needed it!

Of course, I visited with Hettie as often as I could. Like I told you, I've always had a real soft spot for her. She knew she was in plenty of trouble. She needed someone to talk to and just about everybody was staying away from her like the plague.

She'd always had friends. And most of them were happy Thomas Farrington was dead. But I guess they didn't want their friendship or their happiness to show by being around Hettie and maybe getting mixed up in the case.

She was in more trouble than she knew. I couldn't tell her everything, but our evidence was awfully good. We'd found traces of–I can do it when I say it slowly–hex . . . amill . . . something, in her bathroom cabinet. We knew she'd picked up Farrington's pills at the drugstore. And we'd found the, you know–what I just said–in the capsules of the Cardizem bottle in Farrington's medicine cabinet. And then, as everyone knew, Hettie had all those good reasons for wanting Farrington dead.

So I felt real sorry for her in jail. She cried a lot, wouldn't eat much, wouldn't talk to anyone. Didn't matter what I said to her. She'd just ignore me, stare at me but not say anything at all. It was pretty strange. But as I say, I really cared for her and I must have visited her just about every night for a couple of weeks.

Late one night, when we were alone, I asked her whether she would ever speak to me. I said I had a lot of questions like, for instance, whether she had liked Father Berry's cat, which I hadn't. I wasn't examining her or anything similar. It was just my way of trying to be friendly. And it worked, I'll say.

She suddenly broke down, threw herself on her bunk, and sobbed so hard I thought she might get sick. "Loved him . . . I loved that beautiful, beautiful cat!" It seemed to me she would never stop crying. And it made me want to cry just hearing her. There's something about strong people crying. It can break you up.

"It was just a cat," I said.

"Oh God!" she sobbed, and covered her face with her hands. "You're such a dumb little shit! Oh God, God!" She was wailing now.

I looked around, afraid it might bring the temporary cop we'd hired while Dickerson was in the hospital. It didn't though. So I sat on the bench across from Hettie's cell and tried to think things through. How stupid can you be to get handcuffed to a cow? On the other hand, it made me suspicious of Sam Elder. I wondered whether he might have been involved in the cat murder, as I called it. He was certainly strong enough for something like that. And crazy enough, too. It had taken a lot of strength to overpower Silas Coffin and smash up Farrington's body like that. So why weren't we looking into the possibility that Sam Elder was involved in Farrington's murder, as well? Was it because that case didn't involve the use of brute force? Or was it because Sam was supposed to have been in the nuthouse at the time of the Farrington murder? Still, it was worth thinking about. Maybe we'd overlooked something.

Sam was really crazy. All Dickerson did was ask Sam to come to the station so we could fingerprint him. Sam said no and when Dickerson insisted, Sam went berserk. He got his axe out of his tool shed, took

Dickerson's handcuffs away from him and handcuffed Dickerson to the cow. After that he began smashing up his own house with the axe. Even if you're crazy to start with, you don't handcuff people to cows or smash up your own house just because someone wants your fingerprints. Joey had to use his gun to get the axe away from Sam and bring him in for the fingerprinting.

I guess I also had another reason for suspecting Sam Elder. His wife, Marsha, works at the station here. She's a very nice lady. She'd just told Joey the other day that when she talked to Sam in the sanitarium, he'd said some bad things to her. Someone had told him she was sleeping around with people on the island. He was terribly angry and even accused her of doing it with Father Berry!

Marsha didn't want Sam to come home from his sanitarium if he was going to be like that. He could be very threatening, as he was with Thomas Farrington. With Farrington dead, Marsha was afraid Sam's anger would focus on her and maybe her supposed lovers as well. She'd also told Joey she was going to leave Sam, maybe this week. It was a good thing she worked for the police. Joey had even offered her a bunk in one of our spare cells.

Hettie was slowing down on the sobs. I realized—it was kind of a shock for an objective officer of the law—that I was really trying to find almost any excuse I could to get Hettie out of the trouble she was in. I got up and walked to the bars of her cell.

"Please don't cry, Hettie. I'll do all I can for you. Hey, you know some people would say it's a good thing to have a friend in high places on the police force. Number two, as a matter of fact."

She started to giggle. Which made me feel good. I have a reputation for cheering people up, making them smile or laugh. She got off the bed and came to the bars. She was wiping her tears with a tissue. A Scott tissue. We have a pretty classy lockup here. "Maybe you *could* help me, Chick."

I liked the soft way she said "Chick." It's not a name you can usually say softly. "Anything," I said, touching her finger on one of the bars

"Do you ever do any . . . well, private detective work? On your off-time, of course."

I shook my head. "Regulations. I do know them, you know."

She took her hand from the bar. "I see," she whispered.

I couldn't resist asking her what she had in mind. "Nothing," she said. "Forget it!"

"I'd truly like to help you. You know, if I could. I . . . care for you a lot, Hettie . . . though I know you don't care too much for me."

She looked at me and smiled. "That's nice," she said. "I do care for you, Chick. But it really doesn't matter. My goose is cooked, isn't it?"

I told her we had some pretty good evidence. And then I made a big mistake. I broke all the rules. I mentioned the traces of the heart breaker we found in her own medicine cabinet.

She gasped. "That's not possible! No fucking way!" She started having some kind of a fit, beating her hands together and whirling around. "What the fuck! What the fuck!"

"Please, Hettie! Please don't do that!" was all I could think to say. Her language didn't bother me just then. What made me feel so bad was her unhappiness.

After a little, she came back to the bars and put both hands over her heart. "I swear to you, Chick. I swear on my mother's dead body, I swear to Jesus . . . I never saw, never touched any fucking heart breaker. I've heard the name but I can't even pronounce it, for Christ's sake!"

And I'll tell you something. I believed her just then. It wasn't my usual logical self. But it was me, the same person that was doing the logical thinking sitting over there on the bench just now. I believed her! I knew I wanted to believe her, real bad. Her face looked so honest and imploring, her eyes so big and green and pretty. She seemed to be looking straight into my heart.

Maybe she sensed my faith in her. She held one hand out through the bars and I took it. It was real warm and she had nice-looking fingers for a vegetarian and a weight trainer.

"I wanted him dead, Chick. I thought about killing Tommy. God help me, I really did. I even dreamed that one day he'd croak doing a bench press. The bar would fall on his neck and crush his windpipe." She looked imploringly at me. "But honest to God, Chick, I didn't kill him, didn't tamper with his medicines, didn't force him to add weights when I was working with him."

She put her other hand out through the bars and I took that one too. I felt tears in my eyes. "I believe you Hettie. I do, I do! And I'm going to help you. Anything, anything you say!"

Now she was crying again. She took one hand back to wipe her cheeks. "I know it's Father Berry," she whispered. "I know it! I need you to finish my search of his house, the church, his car even. He knows about medicines and drugs and things like that. He even has a bad heart."

"Bad heart? How do you know that?"

She took her hands from mine and put them on the bars. "Some of my clients have–" she looked at me "–have seen him take a nitro for his heart when he was . . . praying and stuff with them."

She seemed to know what I was going to ask. "A nitro is a pill you put under your tongue when you have chest pains, heart pains."

I nodded, as though I'd heard of nitros. But honestly, it seemed weird. Something under your tongue for your heart?

"Could you," she asked, "could we . . . is there a way to get him out of his house so we can really search it?"

"We?" I said. "Maybe you shouldn't be so sure you're going to leave here, Hettie."

She squinted her eyes at me. "I'll get out," she said. "But maybe it would be better if you could . . . would . . . search the house without me?" She put one of her hands out to me again. "I know it's asking a lot, Chick. But if someone saw you with me? Without me, you'd just be doing police work and no one would bother, even Joey."

She squeezed my hands very hard. Those little fingers were strong, I'll tell you. "In spite of what I've said about you, Chick, I do care for you. You're not stupid, really you're not. And just think of the praise you'll get for finding evidence that leads to the real killer!"

About me working alone, there was sense in what she said. She's always been a smart woman. I could be in Father Berry's house for lots of reasons. Investigating Hettie's breaking and entering. Looking for the cat's head. Looking for evidence about Yellow Tie who she said she'd seen. But I'll tell you right now, I didn't really think Father Berry had anything much to do with the Farrington murder. Priests aren't like that. They've got too much to lose. God, for one thing! And besides, I admired Father Berry, even though I'd had that bad morning with him.

But there was someone with an axe trying to get into my mind. You have to honor things trying to get into your mind. I ground my teeth and it came to me. "In the Chief's office," I said to Hettie, "you told me you knew Sam Elder."

She nodded.

"Did the masked man in Father's bedroom look like . . . Could he have been Sam Elder?"

She looked confused. "I really don't—"

"You see, Hettie, I happen to know that Sam might have some crazy idea that his wife and Father Berry . . ."

Hettie looked at me, her eyes big and bright. "That wouldn't be so crazy," she said. "But the man in Father Berry's bedroom—he was wearing a stocking, not a mask—wasn't Sam Elder. I'm sure of that. Sam's not that tall, for one thing. And a yellow bow tie, a suit? He's nuts but not that nuts."

"Just a connection," I said. "About Sam accusing Father Berry. Also he likes to carry an axe and I thought maybe he'd tried to use it on the cat, in spite of what the doc said about its head being torn off."

"Torn off?" Hettie said. She put her hands over her eyes. "Oh God! Torn off? The son of a bitch!"

Just then, Joey walked in from his office down the hall. He often drops in after his dinner, which he usually eats alone across the street at the Atlantic Cafe. "What's going on?" he asked.

"Visiting a little," I said. "She's pretty torn up about the cat."

The Chief looked at me. "You've been visiting quite a bit these last few days. Rather unusual, isn't it?" Then he looked at Hettie. "Three W has a date with Judge Hoguet in the morning. Thinks he can get you out on bail again. I'm against it, of course."

"Budgy will starve without me," Hettie said.

Joey burped and said, "Budgy will starve in hell if he keeps on saying things about me."

"What kind of things?" Hettie asked.

"Lies only you could have told him." The Chief looked at me. "Lies, all of them."

Joey takes a drink with his dinner, I knew that. But it was strange, him talking to Hettie so frank and all in front of me. And what lies was the Chief talking about? Budgy once said in a bar that Joey took bribes. That wasn't true, not at all. Joey did get Christmas presents from certain people. Farrington was one of those people. But the Chief wouldn't have promised anything to Farrington for those gifts, I was sure of that.

There was something strange, though. It occurred to me that Joey was pretty quick to answer the 911s and take care of emergencies himself. Like the way he rushed out to stop Sam Elder from axing down his house. But he never once, so far as I knew, had answered a 911 or gone out of the station to investigate anything that had to do with the Farringtons. It was just a thought, but it stayed with me.

My mind, just then, was on helping Hettie investigate Father Berry. And not getting caught by Joey while I was doing it. "Guess I'll turn in," I said. "Good night, Chief, good night, Hettie. I'll get you those chocolates you asked for."

"Good night, Chick," she said. "I feel much better, thanks to you."

I left them staring at each other. It made me a little blue. As you know, I've always thought maybe Joey might have played around with Hettie years ago before she met her husband. I hoped I was wrong.

It didn't mean anything, of course, but I heard Joey burp and Hettie giggle just before I reached the end of the hall. I felt even bluer about that. Actually, the blue turned kind of black.

CHAPTER NINE

I handed his martini to the man in the yellow tie. "Lovely," I said. "We don't see many of those in our town. Do you tie them yourself?" I was trying my best to be friendly.

He grinned maliciously. With thumb and forefinger he pulled the bow tie forward, let it snap back hard against his gullet. Mockery and malice filled his evil, dark eyes. He was, I knew, an anti-Christ.

He took the glass from me with both hairy hands. The stub ends of his fingers encircling the rim were scarred and dark brown. Had those hands encircled the neck of my dear Saint Augustine, my darling? But this man, Fred Spitzer, Barbara had said, was an old family financial advisor. In spite of his dark, three-piece suit, white button-down shirt, and bow tie, he looked like a mobster to me.

He was big, powerfully built, had broad shoulders and long, dangling arms. His face was pasty under a mass of thick black hair. His eyes were as close to the hairline as eyes can be. They were small and beady over a smashed-in nose just above a small dark mouth. You can understand why, God help me, I'd disliked him instantly.

Of course, I was on edge that day, very anxious, frightened even. It had to do with Sam Elder. I'll explain that in a moment. But this Spitzer fellow, this apelike phenomenon, deepened my fear. Hadn't that meddling Island Life woman told the *Mirror* that the murderer of Augustine had worn a yellow bow tie? Hadn't I very likely prepared an excellent dry martini for my darling's killer?

This was ridiculous, of course. Fear can play havoc with judgement, even the judgement of a clergyman. What I most wanted was to be alone with Barbara, find out where she'd been, tell her my fears.

She'd just that afternoon gotten back from two days somewhere. And just as we were settling down to talk, this Spitzer had arrived. To make matters worse, he had secrets to tell her, needed to be alone with her.

"Oh Ralphie darling," she said after she'd hugged him, "you understand, don't you? Freddie and I need a moment alone, just a *petit soupçon* of a moment."

At my hurt look, she said, "Now it won't be long, dearest. Just the time it will take you to mix Freddie and me two nice martinis." She smiled sweetly at him. "Very dry, straight up, a twist, right?" Then she'd taken him by the hand, led him into the library, and closed the door.

I was angry, of course. What had she to hide from me? We were promised to each other, had vowed on our knees and before God that we would be married. What had this Fred person to say to her that I couldn't also hear?

Thinking of Saint Augustine, I had shaken the martinis ferociously. Barbara well knew how my darling had died. How could she have said "with a twist" to me and in front of Spitzer? Who was this evil looking man she seemed to know so well?

I had then put the shaker down, tiptoed from the terrace bar to the library door. Silence. God forgive me! I put my ear to the keyhole. I heard her say, " . . . hurting me! . . . Take your hands . . ." Then, "Now that's better. You've *never* known your own strength." She laughed. "I'm spoken for, you know. Isn't he just perfect, just right?"

Freddie said something guttural and incoherent. There was silence for a minute. Then a little shriek. Her skirt rustled as she stood. There was unusual anger and command in her voice. "No more of that! You will have a very fast drink and leave, do you understand? You have a truck to pick up, right?"

I hurried back to the terrace, poured the drinks and waited for the two of them. How was I to take those words, "just perfect"? Had there been sarcasm in her voice? Was she simply confirming how much she loved me? And why tell him? What was this thug to her? My mind was in turmoil.

He was now downing his martini in two big gulps, his hairy hands covering the glass. "Good!" he snorted, holding the empty glass out to me.

"Another?" I asked.

"Freddie," Barbara said, running a long red fingernail around the top of her martini, "has to catch the ferry."

Freddie scowled at her, put the glass down. He held his hand out to me. "Meetcha," he grunted. His hand was dry and scaly and much, much too tight around mine. All I could think of was Augustine!

Barbara showed him to the door. When she came back she said, sipping her martini, "Don't ask me anything about him! He's from the past. A friend of Tommy's, really. Not mine."

"I don't like him," I said.

"Neither do I." She put her glass down, her tone changing. "Oh how I love you, darling. How I've missed you!" She put her arms around me, pressed her hips into me. "What's happening?"

I was still angry. "I don't see why you . . . took him into the library without me. What is there to hide from me?"

"Now Ralphie, honey, calm down." She kissed my ear and whispered, "For your benefit, darling. I don't want you to have anything to hide from the police."

I drew away from her. "The police? So he *is* a mobster or something like that?"

"He was working with Tommy. One of the ones who blackmailed him." She handed me her empty glass. "Make me another, please. It was sooo good!"

At dinner I told her almost everything about my day. My anger had subsided, replaced by desire for her. She'd had three martinis by the time we sat down, and some of that physical coarseness I've mentioned was beginning to show. I was pleased the servants had been given several days off.

On the terrace, for instance, she'd been wearing a long, loose skirt and had kept hiking it up, exclaiming how hot the weather was. Then, from time to time, her beautiful legs crossed, she'd run her hand over her thigh and down her calf. She seemed in something of a daze. I had seen that daze before, sometimes even when she wasn't drinking.

Now, in the dining room, she was moving her shoe and ankle against my shin and calf while I talked. It was hard to concentrate. I told Barbara my biggest problem that day had concerned Marsha Elder. She'd come to the rectory without calling for an appointment. She wanted me to know that she had left Sam Elder that very day. She was quite nervous and upset.

Barbara nodded and sliced vigorously into her steak. "Isn't he the one who came after Tommy with a hatchet or something?"

I nodded. "That's the one. Anyway, Marsha Elder and I have been close in the past, and . . ."

Barbara's lips were suddenly tight over clenched teeth. She tapped the knife on the edge of her plate. "You seduced her, didn't you Ralphie? She's one of your persons in high places, isn't she? You get police information from her, don't you? And you screw her now and then, don't you?"

I was flabbergasted. I suddenly remembered I had spoken to Barbara—under duress, at the time—about Marsha as one of my more adoring parishioners, but there was no truth at all in the idea that I had seduced the woman. Common seduction—I call it secular seduction—had never ever been on my mind or in my heart. In any event, Marsha had always resisted my attempts to demonstrate the continuing glories of holy Visitation.

"Don't be ridiculous!" I said with all the force God gave me. I even picked up my napkin, threw it on the table beside my plate. "Honestly, darling. That's very rude of you. Crude, I might add."

"Crude?" she whispered, her eyes as large as her plate. "*Crude?*"

She leveled the knife at me. "Never, never accuse me of being crude! Do you understand that? *Never!*"

"Sorry, darling. Very sorry. It's been a difficult day."

"Just go on with your story," she whispered. "Don't give me that *darling* crap just now!"

It was no use. What I had wanted to tell her, of course, was my fear of Sam Elder. His madness, the sharp axe they say he carried, the mistaken idea he had about Marsha and me. It had been unforgivable of Marsha to come to *me* on the day she had left her deranged husband. There was no way, just now, of telling that to Barbara.

Yes, I had helped Marsha through her troubles. But that was many years ago. Except for this morning's meeting, I'd had no contact with her other than by telephone. Barbara was in no mood to listen to that either.

I had to change the subject drastically. And it had to be a subject Barbara would like. "What's been on my mind," I said truly, "is our wedding and our honeymoon."

"Well, I was going to bring that up, Ralphie, going to bring it up."

She didn't say that in a very kind way, but I could see it had taken her rather inebriated mind off Marsha Elder. "Where would you like–"

"Sicily!" she said immediately. "I have always adored Sicily!"

"Really, darling? With what the Mafia did to ruin Tom's business?"

She put her hand on my knee. "Yes, yes, I know. But the mountains, the seashore, the food, the history. How I'd love to go to Sicily." She looked at me. "And I'll pay for it, darling, the plane fare, first class, the hotels, a driver. We'll have just the right car and driver!"

There was something both sweet and bitter in that reply. She would pay for the trip. That was sweet and not the first time she had understood my budgetary limits. But a chauffeur and a car? That was somewhat bitter. Did she believe I would fail her as a driver? As a map reader? As a conversationalist?

She refilled her glass and mine with wine. "Oh darling, the nights are so beautiful in Sicily, the water so warm. One can go swimming at night, naked. Anything goes in Sicily." Her voice trailed off. "*Mi piacce molto . . . Agrigento, Siracusa . . .*"

Her eyes were closed with memories as she drank copiously of the wine. A bit too copiously, I knew. Barbara, as I've mentioned, could not always manage her alcohol consumption. I thought of another subject. An activity that might not be displeasing to her and that could very well sober her up.

"Your talk of swimming makes me wonder. What about a swim ourselves? It's a very warm night and we could use the exercise."

"Maaavelous!" she said "Jus maaavelous!" She rose awkwardly, almost tipping her chair.

"Could I borrow one of Tom's swimming suits?" I asked. I'd been spending a night or two a week with Barbara but hadn't yet brought more than a change of underwear to the room she'd assigned me down the hall from hers.

"Absolutely no swimming suits," she said, slurring her words.

On the way upstairs I had a chilling thought, but tried to make light of it. "The wiremongers," I said with a laugh, "are they tied up?"

"Oh yes," she laughed back, stumbling up the stairs. "The favorite dogs of that fool policeman are penned, at the moment. Eating each other, poor dears. So hungry."

And at the top of the stairs, she pressed herself into my arms. "I like having them around. I let them loose, but only when you're not here to defend me."

We walked down the beach in sandals and two great white terrycloth robes. I carried a wicker basket with a big beach blanket, two large monogrammed towels, a bottle of champagne–so much for my thoughts of Barbara's sobriety–two champagne glasses and a powerful flashlight.

Outside the house, which was air-conditioned, the night was windless, hot and humid. There was a brilliant harvest moon.

Barbara stopped, removed her robe. Her naked body had never seemed so voluptuous. "Ah," she sighed, "what a perfect night! And what wonderful ideas you have! You're a very reckless man, aren't you Ralphie? For a priest?"

I dropped the basket, took her in my arms, my hands exploring the familiar hollows of her back.

"No, no," she said. "Onward to the sea, the sea! There will be time for everything!"

We spread the blanket on the hard sand at the water's edge, sat down on it while I opened the champagne. The surf was a bit heavy but beautiful as the waves curled, smiled, and broke a few yards from us. The spent water sizzled and sparkled at our feet. In a moment the champagne was sizzling and sparkling in our mouths.

It was then that Barbara laughed and pushed me down on my back. Throwing herself on me, she pressed her mouth to mine and squeezed the Chalice with such force I groaned with pleasure. Champagne instantly ran with gathering force from her mouth into mine. Some of it trickled down my chin and cheek. How blissful! Was this, then, the penultimate, holy exchange of fluids that can overcome the separation of God's children? Was it the spirit of our Lord passing from one of his beings to the other?

Barbara's dyed blond hair glowed in the moonlight. Through the glow I saw Jesus Christ smiling down at us, hands raised in benediction. "Father, Father!" I exclaimed. "Lord Jesus!"

Aware of my exaltation, Barbara turned her head and screamed with terror. Sam Elder stood over us, leering down at us, eyes wild, his axe raised high above his head.

CHAPTER TEN

I didn't see Chick Vado for almost a week. He sent a note through Joey that said, "Still looking for the right chocolates for you, meanwhile working on a crazy big one. Miss you. Chick."

I missed him too, the little wop. His heart was OK. His brain was KO'd, if you know what I mean. Still, I missed him. He'd been coming in every night.

Budgy managed to show up once or twice on visiting hours. He'd stay a while, tell me about this or that match he'd had in Boston or Concord. But he'd wrestled many times in Vermont and liked those bouts the best. His opponents weren't as mean in places like Middlebury and Burlington. There were universities there and even the wrestlers had a few brains as well as big bodies. Of course I wondered whether his little fans, the female kind, had sufficient brains to stay away from *his* big body. I doubted it.

Both times he visited me he was drunk. I gave him all hell for it. He looked sheepish and held my hand and promised to get sober. Then, I was pretty sure of it, he rode the Dresser over to the Pines or the Box to have a few drinks to console himself for making such a promise.

Maybe I was wrong to blame him for that. He was worried about me. And there was plenty to worry about.

Three W had laid it all out for me. The DA would probably try for first-degree murder. He had the evidence—those traces of hexamillathonaroid in my medicine chest—and all the motive he needed. There was nobody else to pin it on, even though the whole town would have enjoyed seeing Tommy dead.

Sam Elder was no longer a suspect. He'd been drugged out on Thorazine in the Falmouth mental lockup until a week after Tommy died. Besides, he hadn't the brains to plant the hexamillathonaroid in Tommy's heart pills.

"Anyway," Three W said, "Sam's toast after what happened yesterday."

"What's that mean?" I asked glumly. I was wondering whether they needed good weight trainers in prisons.

"You don't know the news?" Three W said. "Where you been?" He was smiling of course. The prick! I hoped his cock was still blue and hurt when he got a hard-on.

"It's in the *Mirror*," Three W said. "I doubt they got it right and the Chief's not saying much."

"Come on Wadie," I said. "They don't always include the newspaper when they serve breakfast in this chintzy hotel!"

"Sam discovered Father Berry was visiting Barbara Farrington out at North Point, broke into the house and attacked Berry with an axe. Somebody named Spitzer, a friend of Barbara's, had seen Sam going through the gate—chopping it down with his axe, actually, sparks flying everywhere since it's electrified. Spitzer followed Sam into the house. He says he grabbed Sam from behind just as Sam had his axe raised to finish Berry off. Sam had already sliced into Berry but the blow wasn't fatal. Spitzer cut off Sam's breath until he dropped unconscious. Which is the way Joey and your friend Vado found Sam, almost dead, his jugular and carotids bruised so bad Sponge had to do some quick reconstructive surgery. Might have been better if he hadn't. A quick burial would have cost the taxpayers a whole lot less than keeping Sam locked up for life."

"And Father Berry?" I asked.

"Ran for his life, according to Farrington and Spitzer. Bleeding bad. Police haven't found him yet."

I was surprised and a little pissed at the news. Why hadn't Vado told me about all this? What was Father Berry doing at the Farrington place? Who was this Spitzer hero? "And you don't think the *Mirror* got it right?" I asked.

"Spitzer asked for counsel at the hearing. I interviewed him. Didn't like him, didn't trust him. Parts of his story seemed weird, like Berry running away someplace.

"Spitzer's one of those guys with no past and no present. Couldn't tell me how he knew Barbara, what he was doing out there, what his work was, stuff like that. Dresses funny, too. Pinstriped suit, yellow bow tie and he–"

I grabbed the bars. "The guy in Berry's house. The shit who took the head off the cat!"

"Calm down, honey. I thought of that. Your friend Vado checked it out. Discovered Spitzer had a good alibi. Watching the Sox play ball and plenty of friends to corroborate it."

"Fuck!" I whispered.

"What's that?"

"*Fuck* !" I shouted.

"Oh that," he said.

We talked about whether I was lying about my innocence, and a little about whether I'd get life with or without parole. Then he left me with, "See you, babe. Don't go anyplace without me." I hoped it hurt when he peed, too!

Of course I thought a lot about what Three W had told me. With all the evidence, I didn't think he believed I was innocent. Where the hell was Vado? What had he found out about the chocolates he mentioned, as code I suppose for news about Father Berry? Where was the little runt?

He showed up two nights later. Joey was having his usual dinner at the Cafe. Only that supermoron, Dickerson, was on duty. He was off crutches and walking with a cane now. But wherever he went people were calling him the "cowboy" for his having been handcuffed to a cow. It wasn't very nice, but it's the way things are in our town. People call you all sorts of names behind your back.

So Vado came in with a box of chocolates and a big smile on his face. He put that face right up between the bars. "Good news, Hettie," he whispered. "Good news!"

He looked so boyish, so happy for me, I couldn't resist kissing him. It made me laugh. He practically lost his grip on the bars, started to slide down them. His face was red as a beet.

"Get up, you idiot. Where the hell you been, for Christ's sake? What's happening? What's your news?"

"What's what?" he asked. His face was still red.

"What did you find out, you dumb little runt!" That did it. He swallowed hard, pulled himself back up on the bars but turned his face away from me. There was a tear in his eye. I'd hurt his feelings. "I always called my little brother a runt," I said, patting his hand. "It's an endearment, Chick, just an endearment."

"What's in that box?" a voice said. It was Dickerson, of course. He'd heard our voices and it must have dawned on him that he was on duty.

"A machine gun," Chick said. I could have kissed him again.

Dickerson dropped his cane and drew his .38 from its holster. "That's against the law," he said, his voice cracking.

Chick walked up to him. "Just kidding, friend. Here, take a look." Dickerson looked. "Had me scared, Chick. What kind are they?"

"Bittersweet," Chick said. "The kind Hettie likes."

That was true, but how did Chick know that? "Go on," I said to Dickerson, "help yourself. Good for the brain, you know."

"Gee, thanks," Dickerson said. He took two and started to tell us how his mother had made chocolate cream pies and sold them when he was a kid. "I've got to talk to Hettie," Chick interrupted him. "It's personal. Besides, you ought to get back to the telephone. Lots of crimes going on out there, full moon tonight."

"You handled that just great," I said when Dickerson had limped back to the office.

Chick nodded. "I was just fooling about the machine gun. Can you imagine? Holy Toledo, he pulled his gun!"

"Chick," I said. "Could we get serious now? What did you find out? I've been going a little crazy here."

He put his face back on the bars and whispered, "A check, a check to Father Berry for fifty thousand dollars! I found it in Berry's desk in his office at the church. There was a note with it." Chick fumbled in his back pocket, pulled out a slip of paper. "I copied the note," he whispered. "Look at it yourself. Couldn't trust my memory on a thing like this. In my line of work you've got to know your own weaknesses."

The five words Chick had copied were, *For putting him away. Bobbie*

"Who do you think Bobbie is?" Chick asked.

I didn't answer. *For putting him away?* My heart raced. Was my suspicion about Father Berry confirmed? But with Barbara? Had Berry and Barbara conspired to kill Tommy? Why would they have wanted him dead? Money, of course. Sex? With Father Berry? The idea made me a little sick and I had to think about it. Possibly, yes. Berry and the Holy Ghost were partners in the seduction business. Maybe I had real good suspects, even better than Hettie Hill!

"The way my mind goes on it," Chick said, "is that Bobbie might be short for Barbara." And then, as if in answer to my unasked question, "Farrington was a brute to his wife. Father Berry told me so when I questioned him at his house that time. It wasn't my best day. Didn't take to me, I guess. Said I seemed disturbed."

"Listen to me, Chick. This is important. Tell me what Father Berry said about Barbara. Tell me everything he said."

"Oh, I didn't learn very much. An off day for me. He told me Farrington sometimes left his wife out in the freezing cold, made her beg for a sniff of some drug or other. Is it sniff or snort, I wonder?"

"Sniff or snort?" I said, trying to shake the bars. "What are you saying? Drugs? What's that all about?"

"I'm not supposed to tell you this," Chick said. "But I guess Father Berry wanted us to know Farrington had forced his wife to help him smuggle drugs from some boat or other off North Point. He was a pretty bad man it turns out. I mean even worse than people thought.

What's really crazy is that if the Mafia was involved they didn't bang him down. That medicine, that . . . ah, heart drug did. I just can't pronounce the name of that stuff."

I felt I had just taken that heart stimulant myself. My hands were sweaty and I could hardly get the words out. "Tell me more Chick, much more. What did he say about Barbara, where did Farrington meet her, how long were they married, that stuff. It's vital Chick, real important."

"To tell the truth, I wasn't listening too hard. The cat . . . She was his fourth wife. She was educated at some farm college somewhere. She was very smart and–"

"Some farm college? What's a farm college?"

"Or maybe," Chick said, "it was her diploma. In farming . . ."

Farming degree? I thought. Ridiculous. But just then I got it, I *got* it! "Did you say a farm college. Wait a minute, wait . . . Farm college? Pharmacology? A degree in pharmacology? That's it, isn't it? That's *it*!"

Chick was nodding. "That's right. That's what he said about her. Very good student, very intelligent. She had a degree in pharma . . . what you said. You're real smart yourself, Hettie. Real smart."

I had to sit down on my bunk. I couldn't speak for a moment. I figured Chick thought I was about to faint, but I was wrong. "Sure," he said. "You probably want to get some sleep on that bunk. It's getting pretty late."

"No, Chick honey," I said. "I don't want to sleep again, ever again. If I do, I'll find myself in some fucking prison when I wake up. What I want is Three W. I want him bad. I've got to get out of here. Right away, you hear me Chick? Right away!"

"Sure Hettie, sure you do. But until the trial there's not much chance of that. No, I mean until after the trial. And even then . . ."

"There can't be a trial, Chick. If there is, I'll be history. History, you understand?" I realized I had shouted it out. Which could bring Dickerson again. I walked up to the bars. "Come closer, Chick. Come closer and listen to me. And think hard, please. Think very hard."

I explained that the check Chick found proved that Berry and Barbara Farrington had plotted to kill Tommy Farrington. Her note, signed by Barbara—yes, Bobbie meant Barbara—said 'for putting him away.' 'Him' was Tommy. "Do you understand that Chick?"

Chick was scratching his head. "But Father Berry is a man of the church, a priest. Why would he. . . ?" Then he said "Ouch! Darn fool cat!"

Why the fuck was he thinking about cats? It was hopeless. He'd never get it.

But I went on. "I know he's a priest, Chick. But if Farrington was dead, Barbara would inherit his estate, all his money, and Berry would be a rich priest. Have you got that? A real rich priest, assuming he had a deal with Barbara. Or could get her to marry him."

"Sort of adds up," Chick said, caressing the top of his head. "Must have opened the scab," he mumbled.

"But now listen to this, forget the scab or whatever it is." I told him that someone who knew medicines, prescription drugs, had put the heart breaker into Tommy's capsules. Whoever did it had to know how to put the heart breaker into the capsules and had to know where to get the heart breaker drug. Only someone with a pharmacology background could do that. And Barbara had a degree in pharmacology. So together they killed Tommy. Barbara because he was a brute to her, Berry for the chance to marry Barbara and be a very rich priest. "Do you understand all that, Chicky baby? Do you, honey? Do you?"

Chick looked surprised. My tone had changed with the 'baby' and the 'honey'. I could see the words and my tone had diverted that colossal mind of his. Somewhat. Not nearly enough.

I took another tack. "If you, Officer Vado, were to prove what I've been saying, if you, Police Officer Vado, were to apprehend the murderers of Thomas Farrington, you'd be a hero. You'd be a cinch for Joey's job one day. A cinch for a much bigger salary, be in the newspapers all over the country. Especially since we know now that Farrington was tied up with the Mafia. That's big, baby. That's real big!"

I could see he was thinking it over, smiling a little, looking at me as though he liked what he'd heard. But his face was suddenly troubled. "Everyone hated Farrington, wanted him dead. How would I be a— what you said?"

"The law, Chick, the law. You are sworn to uphold the law. That's what the town needs, that's what the world needs! And you'd be doing it, don't you see?"

He smiled again, but I could see he wasn't swallowing it entirely. So I added, "Smuggling, the beach at night, submarines, dope addiction, wife beating, greed, sex, sinful priests, murder. What the world wants to hear, Chick. National news, Chick, international news!"

He looked at me, narrowed his eyes to show me something important was coming. "There's a development." He looked down the hall toward the office where Dickerson was probably playing with himself. "I didn't tell you, but we had a 911 from Mrs. Farrington last," he concentrated, "Tuesday, I think it was. Late at night. Joey got me out of bed by cell phone and we got out to North Point in fifteen minutes. Well, maybe eighteen or twenty. But fast, siren going the—"

I cut him off. "Chick, please. I don't give a fuck about the siren. Three W told me Sam Elder may have murdered Father Berry and someone named Spitzer tried to save Berry's life. Now they—you, that is—can't find Berry or even his body. Is that true?"

Chick looked disappointed. "That's true." He put a blood-stained handkerchief to the top of his head. "But it's not the development."

"Okay, I'll shut up. What *is* the development?"

"Joey doesn't think it's reverent, but—"

"Relevant," I said and put my hand over my mouth. "Sorry, go on."

"While Joey was questioning the others, he had me watch Sam in the kitchen. Not that Sam was going anywhere. Straitjacket and all, handcuffs on his ankles. He was spitting up water and gurgling and not making much sense.

"But he whispered a whole lot of crazy words. How he was going to kill Berry for what he'd done to Marsha." Chick looked at me confidentially. "Marsha is Sam's wife."

"Jesus, Chick!"

"No, Sam's," Chick said. He lifted the handkerchief from the top of his head and examined it. "Stopped bleeding, I guess."

"Go on, baby, go on!"

"Sam kept saying he found Father Berry on the beach doing it with

Farrington's wife. Well Sam had it wrong of course. Farrington is dead so they're not married any more. But Sam said he went wild when he saw Father Berry doing to Barbara Farrington what Berry'd been doing to Sam's wife.

"And this is really strange. Sam said Spitzer came from the water behind Sam and put some kind of choke-hold on Sam's neck. Next thing he knew he was laying—is it 'laying' or 'lying'?—there in the Farrington kitchen and someone was calling 911, and Barbara Farrington and Father Berry, who'd been, ah, naked on the sand, were getting dressed. I've known Sam all his life, and I think he was really trying to tell me the truth. But I don't get it, Hettie, don't get it at all."

Now my heart was racing like a runaway generator. "I get it, Chick. I get it all right! Barbara and Berry were fucking when Sam discovered them. A lot of people take their clothes off when they do that. Makes things more exciting. Or so I hear."

Chick was red in the face again. Then he stamped his foot and said, "That's still not the development!"

"It's development enough for me," I said. "But go on, go on."

"While Father Berry was dressing, Sam said he heard Spitzer and Barbara Farrington talking about getting stuff off the island and getting off themselves as soon as they could."

Cold sweat was pouring from my armpits. "And Joey doesn't think that's relevant?"

"When Joey wouldn't believe Sam's babbling, Sam went even more crazy, gagging and spitting up water and things. Joey says everybody who has any brains wants to get off this island, including him. Joey says Sam's crazy as a loon, belongs in the mental lockup, and none of what he's said since he handcuffed Dickerson to that cow has ever made any sense. Besides, none of it means anything about who killed Farrington."

I grabbed the bars. "Chick, listen to me now. Joey doesn't know what we know. About Father Berry and Barbara, and the check, and Barbara having that degree. And listen, Chick. If Father Berry and Barbara and this Spitzer get away, get off the island, my little ass is cooked. You get that, Chick? *Cooked!* We've got to stop them, Chick. You and me, honey. And I've got to get out of here. Tonight, you understand. Tonight, baby."

It was rotten of me, I suppose, but what choice did I have? I decided to give him something else to think about. "Listen, Chick. Put your hand through the bars here." I took his hand with one of mine and with the other ran a few fingers up under his cuff. "You're sweet, you know that? I think you're very very very sweet. And smart, too. Very smart. What you've heard from Sam *is* a development, a big one. Joey doesn't see it because he's not as smart as Officer Vado and because he doesn't know what we know."

I pushed his sleeve up and ran my fingers further up above his wrist. "I've always cared for you Chick, I mean it. I'm married you know. But a girl has got to have someone strong and intelligent in her life. Budgy's strong, but, well, he's not always intelligent. You know that and so do I. He's not steady, either. And you are. A police officer, a fine upstanding police officer. Who is also," I scratched Chick's inner elbow, "very sweet, really, really sweet. There is no telling what might happen if . . . well, if you and I together apprehended the Farrington killer, discovered Farrington's connection to the Mafia, were talked about in all the newspapers and television shows. What a pair we'd be, no?"

I pulled his arm through the bars as far as I could and put his hand on my ass. His eyes were big now and he was pressed up against the bars pretty tight below his belt. Before he could get weak again and slip down the bars, I whispered it. "Let me out of here, Chick, right now, tonight. You and I will catch them before they get away. And I promise you, baby, promise you, I'll be yours for the rest of my life!"

His eyes were like big brown saucers. There were little pearls of sweat on his forehead. He shook his head and whispered, "Hettie, Hettie. That would be against the . . . law."

"Put your face up here on the bars, please honey. I want to kiss you, I've got to kiss you!"

He did, and I did, and our mouths fit together just fine. I had him. I *knew* I had him!

CHAPTER ELEVEN

Hettie drove number five, our second police car, to North Point. The force has had five cars over the years. Number five was the last one, a 1984 Chevy, the newest. That left only number four for Joey to use. So I lifted its distributor cap to slow him down. That was Hettie's idea.

And did Hettie ever bitch when she discovered we called this one number five. "What the fuck? We're doomed!" But it was too late. She was behind the wheel and we were half-way out of town.

I don't like admitting it, but I was too sick to drive. There wasn't, according to Hettie, enough time for us to stop so that I could get out of the car to throw up. So I had to stick my head out of the window and let it fly.

I was sick to death. What had I done? Betrayed my trust as a police officer, unlawfully released a prisoner from her cell, stolen a police car. That's what I'd done. I couldn't believe it! I'd be in prison for life, if I wasn't shot and killed by Joey and Rodney and Dickerson who'd be looking for us with guns drawn.

"Stop moaning," Hettie said. "Makes me nervous." I tried to stop. We didn't need her being nervous. We were doing ninety. I'd never get to prison if we hit a deer or went off the road into a tree. Maybe that would be better.

"I've been thinking, Hettie."

"Nice going," she said.

It reminded me of Father Berry saying 'congratulations' in that interview I had with him. I guess it made me mad. I've always tried to control my emotions, of course. Cops have to do that. So I replied, "What you said about Father Berry and Barbara Farrington, does it really add up? Just fu–" I couldn't say it. "Just making love doesn't mean Father Berry and Barbara killed her husband. And the check and the farm degree don't either. Or leaving the island. Sometimes, like right now, I'd like to leave the island too."

The car swerved, fish-tailed, tires screeching. "Son of a fucking bitch!" Hettie said.

"What was it?"

"Rabbit," she said, straightening the wheel. "Baby rabbit."

"Maybe you should go slower," I said, "Might have been a deer."

She sped up. "How we going to get through the fence?" she asked. "Electric, isn't it?"

"Maybe we can't," I said. I was thinking about the wiremongers. "And if we do, there are the–"

"Water's warm," Hettie said. "We could swim around, come in from the beach."

I thought about it. "Hettie?"

"Yeah, baby mine."

"What are we going to do when we get there?"

"You are going to arrest them, honey. You are going to bring them in for suspicion of murder in the first degree."

"I am? Maybe I'm not a police officer anymore."

She put her right hand on my thigh. "You brought your gun didn't you?"

"Forgot it," I said.

She put her hand to her face. "I don't believe it!"

I reached into the glove compartment, pulled out the .38–caliber that's always there.

"Thank God!" Hettie said.

I didn't tell her, but I saw at a glance–I'm a well-trained cop and know how to figure these things–there were no bullets in it. Joey has kept the bullets locked up ever since Dickerson joined the force.

"Hettie," I said.

"Yeah?"

"Do you think we should have told Joey about your ideas, the check and everything, and let him decide what to do?"

"Absolutely not! I know Joey from a long way back. He'd think about it for days and when he finally did something about it, they'd be long gone and yours truly would be in the slammer for life."

"Hettie," I said, "what will Joey do when he finds out we're both gone? I mean Dickerson's going to say I told him to get a cheeseburger while I took over for him."

"They'll think you and I are in love and you helped me escape and we're going to Switzerland or some place like that. Check the ferries, check the airport."

"Not come out here, then?" I said. I was still thinking of those dogs. Maybe they were tied up.

We were at the gate now. It was all smashed up. I'd forgotten that Sam had axed it down without killing himself. Poor Sam in that strait-jacket now, in the lockup on the mainland. He was safe though. I sort of envied him.

Hettie turned out the lights. She knew the place better than I thought and drove slowly around to the back of the big house. It was totally dark, no lights inside. The full moon lit up the outside, weird and kind of blue.

"Looks like they're gone," I whispered.

"Bring the gun," she said, opening her door.

I sighed. "Hettie, there's not any bull–" It was too late. She was out of the car and going down some steps. I got out and followed her down. She was fumbling for a loose shingle, pulled it out and put her hand in. "Got it!" she whispered. She held up a small key.

"You know this place pretty well," I whispered. I knew the rumors about her and Tommy, and I'd been thinking all the way out here about her statement, "I'll be yours for the rest of my life."

She must have guessed what was on my mind. She kissed my cheek. "He's dead, forget it." She put the key in the lock, turned it and then the handle. The door opened with a squeak. "Fuck!" she whispered.

She led the way down a dark hallway lined with boxes. I stopped her and pointed to the label on one of them, *Gracious Homes*. I remembered what Father Berry had told me. "It's what Farrington was smuggling," I whispered.

"She's been doing it all along," Hettie whispered. "But now it's with Berry."

I shook my head. "That isn't what she told Father Berry." Then I thought about it. "Yes, I see, I see." But I wasn't sure I did. Why had Father Berry told me what Mrs. Farrington had told him about smuggling? It didn't, just then, add up for me. But I was pretty scared. A gun with no bullets and I was supposed to make an arrest?

There was a sound, like a moan, from down the hall. We went further and saw a small streak of light from under a door to our left. We listened for a minute or two. It was a man's moan. There were little gasps for breath in between the moans.

"Your gun," Hettie whispered. "We're going in."

"Hettie, I want to tell you something."

"Later," she said. She pulled back the bolt on the door, flung it open.

The room was big with track lighting. An exercise room, a gym with barbells and weights, a treadmill, and all kinds of Nautilus stuff. Facing us, sitting on a rowing machine, gagged, his arms and legs clamped to the machine, was someone who looked a lot like Father Berry.

I put the .38 in my pocket and we removed his gag and freed him from the clamps, which had cut into his wrists and ankles. "Thank the Lord," he groaned and his head went sideways as though he would faint.

Hettie went to a water cooler and brought back a full paper cup and a towel. She wet the towel and washed his face and let him drink a little.

When he looked as though he could understand me, I pulled the .38 from my pocket and said, "Sorry, Father, you're under arrest. You have the right to remain silent but . . ." I reached into my back pocket for the required message.

Hettie put her hand on my shoulder. "I had it wrong, Chick. Had it wrong."

Father whispered, "They will be back. Monsters! They're monsters!"

"Where," Hettie said, "are they?"

"Right here," Barbara Farrington said from the door. "We're right here!" She held a little automatic pistol in her hand.

The man standing next to Barbara was holding a sawed-off shotgun. He wore —I took it all in at once—a pinstriped suit and a yellow bow tie, both of which reminded me of something important. He had long arms, an ugly face, and very bushy black hair. He looked at me and said, "Drop the gun mouse. Drop it or I'll blow your head off."

I dropped it. When it hit the floor, it went off, spinning around like a top. Everyone jumped. Mouse, was I? He'd pay for that!

"You!" Hettie said. "You blow heads off people and you rip heads off cats. You're a fucking, ugly bastard!"

"Freddie!" Barbara screamed. It was too late. Yellow Tie hit Hettie so hard she crashed back against the wall and slid to the floor. She started to get up. "You shithead gorilla!" He walked over to hit her again and I went crazy. You don't think about those things. I threw my body into the back of his knees. He crumpled and his shotgun slid across the floor.

Barbara put the automatic in her belt and picked up the shotgun. She held it as though she knew how to use it. "All right now, everybody. Get back to where we were, or this Christer who thinks a dick is a Chalice, will die right now!" She put the barrel of the shotgun in Father Berry's mouth. In a ladylike voice she said, "Oh Ralphie, darling, I just can't bear to see you looking so frightened like that."

Yellow Tie began to laugh. He stood, turned and picked me up. By the neck. "Knock Spitzer down, eh?" As he laughed I could see several of his gold teeth and the pink back of his throat. My feet were off the floor and I couldn't breathe. So I opened my eyes and mouth as wide as I could and gurgled. Then I closed my eyes and went limp. It wasn't that hard to do.

When Yellow Tie dropped me, I stayed dropped. I kept my mouth open and my eyes closed. That was hard to do, as scared as I was.

For some reason, Barbara Farrington was pleading. "I've got to have one, Freddie. You promised, and this is too much, too much!"

"We'll have them load the truck," he mumbled.

"Not if you keep beating them up," Barbara said. "Please now, Freddie, another fix, or I swear I'll blow you to bits!"

Freddie laughed and I could hear a door open, a drawer pulled out, little clicks of metal on glass. I could also hear Hettie crying. It tore me up.

"Give me the gun," Yellow Tie said.

"No, Freddie." She giggled. "You're too impulsive. A fiend." There was silence. Then Barbara sighed. "Ah, that's it, that's it. So good, Freddie. You're saving my life."

"But not theirs," Yellow Tie said. "We've agreed to that. Haven't we?"

"Darling Freddie," Barbara said. "Just not here. They should be a special treat for the—"

Spitzer laughed that deep way of his. "The dogs," he said. "Did you hear that, you there mouse?"

I guess he kicked me. A sharp pain in my ribs. I tried not to yell out or open my eyes. Then Yellow Tie must have hit Father Berry. I heard him cry out with pain. "The dogs!" he yelled out again. "Hungry, very hungry! And they eat everything, bones, head, everything!"

"Fuck you!" Hettie said. And he hit her again. I could hear his fist crack on her head somewhere. Why couldn't she keep her mouth shut.

I thought I heard the sound of a motorcycle. Then I knew I did. No one spoke as the motor cut out. A door creaked somewhere and there was the sound of boots coming along the hall. Could it be Joey? But the force didn't have a motorcycle.

"Where are you? Where are you?" It was a high-pitched voice, more a squeal than a shout.

"Budgy!" Hettie said. Then she screamed out, "Run, Budgy. Guns, they have guns!"

Barbara Farrington must have gone into the hall to meet him. I heard her say, "I told you not to come until I called you! You fat fool!"

Budgy squealed, "But you promised, you promised! You're running away from me. You're leaving me, aren't you?" He was sobbing. It sounded like the weeping of a little child.

They must have come back into the room. "Hettie!" Budgy screeched.

"What's that mean," Hettie whispered, "'until I called you'?"

Budgy didn't answer her. Instead there was a crash of bodies, the sounds of a wall cracking, a Nautilus machine overturning, screams of pain, great grunts and gasps for breath, curses and groans. Barbara Farrington was shrieking, "Stop it! Stop it you fools!"

Now was my chance. I rose fast, dizzy and blinded by the light. I slammed the hall door shut, bolted it, ran down the hall to the outside door Hettie and I had come through. I shut it and turned the key in the lock. I climbed the stairs and got into number five just as the dogs lunged at me. Howling, snapping, they looked more like skeletons of dogs, their matted, gray hides streaked with scars. I caught the nose of one when I slammed the door shut. It screamed with pain.

The keys were not in the switch, not under the seat, not in the glove compartment. I found them in the sunscreen above the driver's seat. I was wondering why Hettie had put them there. But I didn't wonder long. Yellow Tie was this moment beating down the cellar door I had bolted, would follow me up the stairs, try to kill me with one of the guns they had. Two of the dogs were now on the hood of the car, their claws sliding, their pink eyes crazed, their huge open jaws drooling over the windshield. One of them ripped a wiper from its post.

I started the engine, turned the car in the direction of the gate. The dogs kept up with me, swerving in front of the car as though to cut me off. I hit one of them, a terrible crunch, and almost lost control of the car.

I switched on the radio, couldn't remember the words. "Mayday!" I yelled into the mike, "Mayday, mayday!" What good would that do?

So I said, "Joey, it's me, if you're listening. And if you're not listening, Joey, you won't know where I am. And I'm in number five and dogs are chasing me and they got Hettie and Father Berry and, listen Joey, we need you bad."

There was still something missing. And just before I saw the white truck with *Gracious Homes* written on the side, I yelled into the mike, "Farrington place, Farrington place!"

Sitting in the cab of the truck—I couldn't believe it—was Yellow Tie. I could see the tie, I could see his grinning face, I could see the rifle he was holding, I could see the gun was aimed at me, and, Holy Toledo, it was firing at me. I heard one of the headlights bust into pieces. The wheel wrenched around in my hands and I was sure my wrist was broken. I was a goner, I knew that. My career, my life, my love for Hettie, my life in prison was over. But I tried to save myself. I hit the brakes, missed the pedal and hit the accelerator instead. The car surged forward, hit another dog, swerved and smashed into the truck and everything went black.

CHAPTER TWELVE

T wo years have elapsed since the end of my selfless efforts to save Barbara Farrington's soul. And how frightfully my labors ended: two nights and days during which I was almost murdered by Sam Elder and then by Fred Spitzer and Barbara herself!

At the time, I could not believe such horrors could possibly happen to me, a man of the cloth, devoted to the service of my parishioners, ambitious to spread the good news of Jesus to my island and, yes, to the world at large. All my intentions had been honorable and moral, my work salutary and effective. Why would God have permitted my life and career to be so jeopardized?

After months of meditation and prayer, I now have the answer to that question. But to fully understand the answer, you must know what has happened to me and others from the time of the horrors themselves until this very day.

You can imagine my terror, my certainty that God's final judgement was only seconds away, when I saw Sam Elder standing over us. The number of those seconds depended only on the time it would take for Sam's raised axe to split my skull, assuming the axe did not first cleave Barbara's. She had, perhaps unfortunately, rolled out of our holy embrace as Sam made that last, quick upswing that would assure the maximum downward velocity of his axe.

As the downswing commenced, I saw a huge, hairy hand and a pinstriped sleeve encircle Sam's neck. The grip cut off Sam's shriek of surprise and rage as it pulled him backward and down into the water. I sat up, covered my shrinking Chalice with my robe. Fred Spitzer, up to his knees in the surf, was holding Sam's bald head under the foaming water while Barbara screamed, "No Freddie! No!"

Only when Sam's legs stopped churning did Freddie –grinning with evil satisfaction–drag Sam to dry land. Then it was that my beloved Barbara said the most astonishing words: "Darling Freddie, you've saved my life again!" Her life?

And my beloved's actions were equally heartbreaking. Entirely naked, unabashed, she flung her arms wide, clasped that evil anti-Christ to her body while he roared with laughter and clawed at her buttocks. Bitter phlegm rose in my mouth. Only minutes before it had been filled with champagne from Barbara's lips. How cruel, how devastating life can suddenly become!

They both turned to look at me. Barbara said to Spitzer–she was so cruel, so wicked–"You should have let the axe fall, Freddie." This from a woman who had loved me, given me her entire self, donated fifty thousand dollars to my parish for my services in putting her husband out of her troubled mind.

Spitzer laughed maliciously at her suggestion about the axe. "Whenever you wish it to fall!"

Sam Elder groaned, coughed; water spewed from his nose and mouth.

"That maniac," Barbara said with disgust, "has changed everything."

"Not everything," Spitzer leered. He had begun clawing her with both hands.

"Not now, you idiot! Get away from me. I have to think." She put on her robe, told Spitzer to get Sam's axe, bobbing and turning in the surf.

When he waded into the water, I said, "Barbara, in the name of our Lord, what is this all about?"

She laughed. "It *was* about marrying you. Now it's about disposing of you!"

Was it with compassion, some leftover feeling of love for me, or was it simple cunning that now caused her to say, "I really hadn't planned to kill you, Ralphie darling, unless you did something stupid. Which," she laughed again, "you probably would have done."

Spitzer was back with the axe, his suit soaked with water.

"Bring it," she said, running her finger over its cutting edge. "I know what we'll do."

They ordered me to drag Sam's body, feet first, over the sand and lawns to the house. Puffing and wheezing, I could only hear them when they came back to help me jerk Sam over a curbstone or up a steep incline. They spoke of a *Gracious Homes* truck Spitzer had brought to North Point that very night. They whispered other things that chilled my heart: " . . . load the stuff . . . Montreal . . . Jesus in the cellar . . . cut him bad . . . murder . . ."

We entered the house by the kitchen door. Spitzer stood guard over Sam while Barbara permitted me, at gunpoint, to dress. I pleaded for my release but to no avail. She said I would definitely be released entirely, very soon, but in the meantime she had a cozy place for me to spend my last hours.

The cozy place was a huge, well-lighted gymnasium of some kind. It was to be my prison for hours of constant torture and terror.

The first night, the night they called the police, I was certain I'd be killed at any minute. How nearly right I was! I learned later that Spitzer and Barbara convinced Joey Horne that I had fled, mortally wounded by Sam Elder, who, when they found my body, should be charged with murder in the first degree. I heard the footsteps of the police and doors opening and closing above me, but I was so tightly gagged I could scarcely breathe, much less shout for help.

I have never understood why they chose to keep me alive for the next forty-eight hours. Had Barbara Farrington, monster that she was, retained some sentimental feeling for me? Were they planning to use me as a hostage if their escape went awry? Did they, in their perversions of pleasure, need an audience? During that period, they clasped me to one or another machine in the room, brought me water and small cans of the most frightful spaghetti with meat sauce. I had to beg them to let me go to the toilet and to give me additional water. The painful clasps and clamps they used were inventions, Barbara told me, of her late lamented husband. "The bastard," she said, applying a clamp to my leg. "He taught me the pleasures of cocaine and used me like a slave."

During the day I listened to them loading a truck. Once in a while I heard it start up and leave the premises. Those were my better hours. The evenings were my worst. One late afternoon they fastened me to a rowing machine, forced me to row while they drank wine, fondled each other, injected themselves with drugs that made them wild with laughter while they performed sinful sexual acts. May God forgive me for what I saw.

You can well imagine my utter joy and relief when Police Officer Chuck Vado and the Island Life woman, Mrs. Hill, came to my rescue. I had always held them both in high regard. And how brave they were after Spitzer and Barbara discovered their presence. Even Spitzer did not frighten Mrs. Hill—Nettie is her name—though she paid a serious and painful price for telling the beast what she thought of him. He hit her twice and so terribly hard any normal woman, or man for that matter, might well have died.

That was when Chuck Vado so courageously threw himself into Spitzer who proceeded to pick the little man up by the neck. I have never seen such hands as Spitzer's, the shape and efficiency of steel vices. Chuck was rendered unconscious in seconds.

When we first heard the high-pitched voice of Budgy Hill, Nettie's husband, we thought we might be saved. How terribly Nettie suffered when she learned the truth. I know I suffered. Budgy was one of my special Christian tasks, a very mixed-up human being whose demons I had so long tried to exorcise. Could he have sent that telegram, from some remnant of Christian love, to warn the police that Thomas Farrington was going to die?

But it was immediately clear from what he said and did when he first entered the gym that he had made an alliance with the Devil. He and Barbara Farrington—I had suspected it more than once—had been having an illicit and immoral affair, trysting for many months, perhaps years, in Vermont cities where he'd told us he'd been having a series of successful wrestling matches.

It took Budgy a moment or two to realize that Barbara was leaving him for Spitzer. But then, ignoring Barbara's shotgun, Budgy squealed like a stuck pig and charged into Spitzer with demonic fury.

We witnessed then the most remarkable and vicious battle I have ever seen. Eye gouging, ear tearing, blood spouting from great bites taken out of faces, necks, and hands. They swayed together like some huge, bellowing animal, then flipped and rolled and kneed the other in belly and crotch. They shouted, screamed with rage and frustration, spewed saliva and blood, spit teeth on the floor, smashed each other down so hard the walls shook around us.

It was, of course, those vice-like hands of Spitzer's that finished Budgy. Not by strangulation, Budgy had no neck. But at various times during the battle Spitzer simply broke one or another of Budgy's fingers until all ten were broken, ripped, and bleeding. The crack of the bones and Budgy's screams of pain will resound in my ears forever. And I had no doubt, just then, who had hacked the fingers off the dead body of Thomas Farrington.

When Budgy fainted, Spitzer began stomping Budgy's face and neck. At that moment, there was a sharp slam of the gym door. Miracle of God's miracles, Officer Vado had revived and even then was running for the police car he and Nettie had brought to North Point.

Barbara screamed and blasted the door with her shotgun. The two terrible sounds of it frightened me. I was certain my heart would stop beating. Spitzer charged the door like a bull. It burst open and Barbara shrieked, "The truck. Take the truck! And kill him! Kill him!"

It was Nettie, not I, who understood guns sufficiently to risk a sudden attack on Barbara. The two shotgun blasts had, she told me later, exhausted the chambers of the gun. And screaming like an avenging angel, she rushed Barbara and hit her hard on the chin. Barbara staggered back, slipped on the floor—covered as it was then by sweat, saliva, blood, and the other remnants of Budgy and Spitzer's battle.

Even so, Barbara pulled the pistol from her belt. Nettie swung again and Barbara dropped unconscious to that slippery floor.

Within minutes we had attached Barbara to a machine Nettie said was appropriate. She called it the Farrington Hard-on Lat-pull, a reference I did not until later fully understand. (I will return to part of that reference in these pages.)

With incredible effort, we dragged the traitorous and still unconscious Budge between two large adjacent machines and clamped him securely to them. Nettie found his gold bridge among the broken teeth on the floor and, not unkindly, put it back in his mouth. We then searched frantically for additional shotgun shells, found them upstairs, loaded the gun, cocked Barbara's and Officer Vado's pistols, and waited for Spitzer's return.

As everyone knows, Fred Spitzer did not return. The incredible courage and skill of Police Officer Vado, now Sergeant Vado, was responsible for the demise of that evil anti-Christ. The *Mirror* and other New England newspapers reported—confirmed by our Police Department—that Chuck, confronted by Spitzer at the North Point gate, dodging bullets and a horde of vicious dogs, rammed his police car into Spitzer's truck in such way as to spring open both its doors. It was the *Gracious Homes* truck Spitzer and Barbara had been using to transport drugs. Spitzer had taken it to cut off Vado's escape.

That officer, those reports said, had to calculate precisely the point of impact that had the greatest likelihood of springing open one or both of the doors of the truck. He was courageous enough, as well, to risk his own life in ramming his police car at top speed into the truck to effect his intended result. He knew, of course, that when the doors opened, the North Point dogs, vicious and trained to kill, would drag Spitzer from the truck.

Unconscious from the frightful collision—not wearing a seat belt, the *Mirror* admonished—Officer Vado did not have the satisfaction of witnessing his success. But both truck doors did spring open, the dogs leapt in and dragged Spitzer out of the truck to the ground.

A thorough search by the police produced shreds of pinstriped material leading to a small pile of splintered bones, human viscera, and canine excrement. Nothing more of Spitzer was ever found. With one odd exception. Near the little pile, on the green, well-manicured lawn, there lay a clean, ready-to-wear, yellow bow tie.

After their repast, the dogs escaped North Point through the broken gate. They were, for many months, considered a threat to our community. To assure our safety, the police destroyed the last of the North Point dogs in October. Whether from chronic indigestion, lack of appetite, or distaste for local flesh, none of the dogs ever attacked an islander.

May I turn to another subject? As I've said, two years have gone by since the Farrington debacle. And I have often asked myself why my career and my very life could have been so jeopardized by the events of that period. The answer, I believe, is simply this: through danger and risk and pain, the Lord God Almighty brings us security and happiness.

Let me give you concrete examples from these very pages. Nettie Hill had been married to Budgy Hill whose immoral and illegal activities caused her no end of embarrassment and pain. As you know, she was charged with the murder of Thomas Farrington. In proving her innocence, she risked great dangers, rid herself of Budgy Hill, and now owns two additional health clubs, one on the Vineyard, the other in Hyannis.

Or take Chuck Vado, one of the finest policemen I have ever encountered. He risked prison and his life to free Nettie Hill from our island jail. He confronted two dangerous and pathological criminals, a horde of vicious and hungry dogs to maintain order and justice on our little island. His reward was national recognition, a ten-percent increase in salary, and promotion to the rank of sergeant.

Finally, take my own case. I risked incredible dangers, suffered unbelievable pain resulting from my selfless counsel to Budgy Hill and Barbara Farrington. Had I not been their priest and selfless advisor, would Fred Spitzer now be dead or Barbara Farrington and Budgy Hill in prison for life? The answer, of course, speaks for itself.

Nor would I have been free to court my darling Marsha who, upon Sam's demise in prison, inherited his sizable—and exceedingly valuable—

acreage on the South Shore of our island, leaving her free to marry me just this last year.

And something more. Is it indiscreet of me to add in confidence that I am now taking a slight variation of hexamillathonaroid, called hexamillat, for the remarkable effect it has on the holy Chalice? You may remember the erectional side effect an overdose of hexamillathonaroid had on Thomas Farrington just before and just after his death. Dr. Langor, "Sponge," as we call him, and I have discovered that this variation of hexamillathonaroid does not have that drug's fatal characteristic and is considerably more effective than the now famous Viagra. It produces results almost instantly and enlarges the male member by an average of 35.7 percent above its customary fully erected length and circumference. Several well-known pharmaceutical companies are bidding for our patent rights.

We are not inclined to sell. The new owner of North Point, Mr. Carmine Reale, has suggested his international organization would be interested in financing our development, production, and marketing of the drug. Mr. Reale became a devout parishioner of the Heavenly Rest in converting from Roman Catholicism. He is highly respected by our island's residents, has made many good friends here, including Chief Joey Horne, and is running for selectman on our April ballot.

Speaking of connubial matters, I should tell you about my dear Nettie and Chuck. That's correct. Nettie's divorce came through in March and I look forward with great pleasure to marrying these two lovebirds next Saturday afternoon at the Heavenly Rest. That's my church, of course, now broadcasting from our little island to the entire country on National Public Radio.

May God's wonders never cease! Amen.